Diablo
to the rescue

Gabi Adam

Diablo
to the rescue

Copyright © 2002 Gabi Adam
The story and the names of the characters are fictional.
Original title: Diabolo, Lebensretter auf vier hufen
Cover photo: Bob Langrish
Cover design: Stabenfeldt AS/Elsebeth Christensen
Translated by Barclay House Publishing
Edited by Karen Pasacreta
Printed in Germany, GGP Media GmbH 2002
ISBN 82-591-0863-1

*For all young riders who dream of owning
their own horses.*

Chapter 1

When Ricki went to bed on Christmas Day evening, she was convinced she'd be unable to sleep. She was still excited by the events of the past few days—the good and the bad—and she just couldn't believe that, as of today, Diablo belonged to her. She knew she had Jake to thank for that. And she vowed to herself: *Anyone who calls Jake a bad-tempered old weirdo will have to answer to me.*

The stable master had managed to convince Ricki's father that it was not the horses' fault that her grades were bad. But Jake had said nothing about what the real reason was, and Marcus had remained silent on that subject as well.

At any rate, Ricki had not been forbidden to go to the stables, as she'd expected; instead, she'd been given *her own horse!* Unbelievable! Sometimes parents can be hard to understand. Ricki avoided talking about it to her father. There was always the slim possibility he would change his mind and sell Diablo.

In any case, she was now a brand-new horse owner. Jake had given the black gelding to her as a present after clearing it with her father. Jake's only condition was that he be allowed to remain near Diablo for the rest of his life. After all, he had reared the horse. *As far as I'm concerned, he can sleep in Diablo's stall every night, if he wants to,* thought an ecstatic Ricki. She closed her eyes and imagined herself galloping over the meadows and fields on the black horse. "Thank you, dear Jake," she mumbled as she drifted off to sleep.

*

Ricki was one of those teenage girls who was entirely fascinated by horses. Up until now, her schoolwork had been only half as important to her as the time she spent at the riding academy.

Like a lot of 13-year-old girls, she had been dreaming of owning her own horse for ages. Whenever she and her friends Lark and Cathy sat in the gallery at the academy and stared down at the riders performing in the ring, they imagined that they were among them. Of course, they agreed that they would do things a lot differently from the way these present owners did them. The girls were outraged over the use of spurs and the fact that many horses were forcibly made to jump over barriers.

They were especially upset with Frank Cooper, who had often mistreated Diablo and believed he had a right to beat his horse into submission. "These animals are very stupid," he was often heard to say.

Strangely, the board of trustees of the riding academy had never enforced their code of conduct regarding the treatment of horses on Cooper. Probably because he donated a lot of money to the riding club. But no matter what happened in the past, from now on, Diablo would never again be mistreated; now he was in Ricki's care.

The next morning she woke up early feeling excited and refreshed. For one terrible moment, she thought perhaps she had dreamed it all. But when she saw the bit that Jake

6

had given her hanging over the chair, she knew that her dream was indeed a reality. She wanted to get up immediately, but sank back on her pillow with a groan. "Oww!" she winced. In her excitement she forgot about her injured collarbone. A piercing pain shot throughout her body. What a nuisance! She finally had her own horse, and she couldn't even take care of him, much less ride him. She knew Jake would take good care of Diablo. And, in the meantime, Diablo needed time to recover from Cooper's ill treatment before beginning a schedule of training with a rider on his back.

Ricki looked up at the ceiling. So many thoughts crossed her mind—school, her grades, the prospect of being forbidden to go to the stables, the ugly fight with her mother. When Ricki remembered it all, she felt sick. What had she accused her mother of? Oh, yes, that her job kept her so busy she never had any time for her children, that she was never available when Ricki needed her, and so on. In the meantime, without telling her family, Brigitte Sulai had decided that after her two-week Christmas vacation from her job, she would resign permanently as soon as a replacement could be found.

Ricki hadn't said anything about it yet, but she was acutely aware that in her time of crisis her mother had been there for her every minute. She came to the conclusion that her parents weren't the worst parents in the world, and she had probably gone overboard in some of her criticisms. *Growing up just isn't that easy*, Ricki sighed. But as soon as she thought about Diablo, her face beamed. She was sure that any problems that came up with him, real or imagined, would be easily solved.

I have to call Lark and Cathy, she thought. She chuckled to herself when she imagined their incredulous looks when she told them she was Diablo's new owner. *Better not to call them,* she decided quickly. *I want to see their reactions firsthand.* Lark and Cathy would probably be at the riding academy today anyway, as they were every day. Ricki hoped her parents would drive her to the stables, since she couldn't ride her bike because of the accident. Then she would have the opportunity of telling her friends the wonderful news face to face.

After an hour of lying in bed and thinking over the recent events, Ricki heard a noise outside her room. She got up carefully, opened the door quietly, and looked out into the hallway. Light shone at the end of the hallway from the door to the kitchen below. It was still pretty cold in the house at this hour in the morning, so Ricki hurried back into her room to get her bathrobe and draped it around her shoulders.

Then she went down the stairs and stood in the doorway to the kitchen. Her mother, still in pajamas, had already set the table for breakfast and was filling the thermos with freshly brewed coffee when she noticed her daughter.

"Good morning, Ricki. What are you doing up at this hour? Can't the new owner of Diablo sleep any longer?" she asked, smiling.

"Sort of," yawned Ricki. "I've been awake for an hour and thought I heard a prowler down here, so I decided have a look in the kitchen.

"Would you like some coffee?"

"I thought coffee was only for adults."

"Well, I think we can make an exception this one time. It's early and you're already up, and you are on vacation. I imagine—"

"Yeah, yeah, Mom, give it to me!" Ricki grinned. "You wanted to say that during school I'm nervous enough, and you didn't want to make it any worse, didn't you?"

8

Mrs. Sulai laughed, but at the mention of school she thought back to the fight she'd had with Ricki about her poor grades.

"Ricki, I think we should talk," she began hesitantly, afraid that Ricki would become defensive and leave the room if this subject was brought up again too soon. But surprisingly, Ricki sat down on the round stool near the cupboard. Before her mother could say anything else, Ricki interjected: "Mom, I'm sorry about what I said to you, you know, about your job and stuff. I was just depressed. I wanted to tell you this a few days ago, but it never seemed like the right time. I've thought about it, and you don't have to quit working on my account. That was just stupid of me. Really."

"Look what having your own horse can do." They heard a deep male voice from the doorway. Ricki's father was up too.

"Did I hear correctly? Your mother may continue to work?"

"As far as I'm concerned, yes," nodded Ricki, grabbing a handful of Christmas cookies out of the large tin on the counter.

"And what about me?" Marcus looked at his wife, pretending to be angry. By way of an answer, she handed him a mug of hot coffee.

"Well, you guys, actually I wanted to wait until the whole family was together around the breakfast table, but waiting for Harry is probably a waste of time. He doesn't get up before 10 a.m. during vacation. What I wanted to tell you all is that I have handed in my resignation effective as of February 15. I couldn't do it any earlier because they have to find someone to replace me."

Ricki and her father stared at Brigitte in silence. They

9

never thought she would give up her job, which she loved so much.

Since no one said anything, Mrs. Sulai, slightly amused, continued, "Well, you're not exactly jumping for joy. Had I only known. Also, that was supposed to be my Christmas present for everyone, but then Diablo stole the show. I hope you—"

"Wow, super! You're really going to stay home?" Ricki broke in, visibly happy about her mother's decision. Marcus gave his wife a hug.

"I totally agree with my daughter. After all, I never wanted you to work in the first place."

"Yeah, I know, and that's probably the reason I did it," Brigitte admitted.

Marcus gave her a kiss made of coffee, cookies, and powdered sugar. She tried to get out of his arms, laughing, while Ricki, sipping her very light coffee, just enjoyed the playful family atmosphere. It hadn't been like this in a long time.

"May I disturb you two a minute?" Ricki asked politely. "Could someone drive me to the stables today? I can't ride my bike yet." She pointed to her bandage.

"Of course, my daughter," her father answered gallantly. "I thought that you'd probably like to say good morning to Diablo—that's why I got up so early. But don't think I'm going to do this every day," he added.

Ricki was ecstatic. She hopped off the stool, and gave her father a quick hug. Forgetting about her pain, she ran upstairs to get dressed. She was back in the kitchen barely five minutes later. How she had managed to get dressed so quickly despite the bandage, seemed like a miracle to her! Thinking about Diablo gave her wings in every sense of the word.

"I'm ready. As far as I'm concerned, we can leave now," she said.

Her father looked down at his sweat pants. "Maybe I should get dressed too. Otherwise everyone will think that I had to pawn my clothes to buy my daughter's horse." Although he sensed that his daughter could hardly wait to see Diablo, he drank the rest of his coffee and then used up quite a lot of time in the bathroom shaving. When he was finally finished, Brigitte found him very handsome, but Ricki said, "Diablo would have recognized you shaved or unshaved." Finally they could leave for the stables.

"Will you two be back for lunch, or aren't you sure when you'll be back?"

"We'll see—we'll try to be back in time," Marcus replied, and winked.

"Bring Jake with you," Brigitte called after them. As Ricki headed out the door into the frosty morning, she gave her mother a thumbs-up sign that let her know she understood.

Ricki's father drove slowly out of the garage. This morning the streets were dangerously icy, and they needed extra time to get to the riding academy.

Ricki had opened the car door even before it came to a full stop. And she had disappeared inside the entrance before Marcus had locked up.

"Good morning, Jake!" she called merrily and gave him a kiss on the cheek as she ran on past. "How's Diablo? Has he survived his late-night visitors?"

Jake beamed. He was glad to see Ricki so soon. When he saw how excited she was to see her horse, he knew he had done the right thing in giving Diablo to her. "Good morning, Ricki. Diablo's fine. See for yourself."

Ricki felt bad about rushing past Jake, but she couldn't help it. She just had to see her horse. And Diablo must have felt the same, for he nodded his head when he saw her and nickered a greeting.

11

Marcus greeted Jake heartily and struck up a conversation, while Ricki got the currying comb out of her basket. With only her good arm, she tried to make Diablo's coat shine, but it wasn't easy. Awkwardly, she carried on with the grooming tools. She had to be careful not to make any hasty movements with her upper body. She held the comb with the hand of the arm in the sling and brushed with the other over Diablo's coat. Every time she cleaned the brush on the comb, a huge dust cloud coated the white sling that covered her arm.

Marcus observed his daughter, admiring her at work. He thought of Frank Cooper, the man responsible for her injured condition, and felt his hatred return. Just then Jake gently rested his hand on Marcus's shoulder.

"I know what you're thinking," the stable master said softly. "You can imagine how often I see those images in my dreams. I see that man beating Diablo in his stall, and I see Ricki desperately trying to stop him from abusing the horse. I feel your daughter's pain as Cooper's rage concentrates on her, and he hits her with the metal bit until she collapses." Jake looked directly into Marcus's eyes. "Don't think it's easy for me to bear this memory. I feel so guilty that I couldn't help her."

"But you did help her! After all, you went after him with the pitchfork, and—"

"Yeah, yeah, but Ricki was already lying on the floor. It's so depressing to be old and unable to react as quickly as you want to."

The two men stared at each other in silent understanding.

After Cooper's mistreatment of Diablo, Jake had bought the horse for the symbolic price of one dollar from the animal-protection group that had commandeered Diablo from his brutal owner. He'd given the horse to Ricki because he was convinced it was best for Diablo. He also hoped that with Diablo to care for, Ricki would be able to better cope with her awful experience with Cooper.

Marcus, on the other hand, was glad that his daughter was so much better—the broken collarbone would heal—and that she was so happy with Diablo.

After a while Diablo's coat began to shine, and his owner's white sling had turned gray. The horse looked at her closely, and he whinnied loudly. It seemed he was laughing at Ricki, who was making the weirdest movements in order to avoid any pain in her shoulder while grooming Diablo.

"Yeah, yeah, okay. I got it. You're fine, your coat is shiny, and I look like a pig! You think that's funny?" Lovingly, she patted the neck of the black horse and left a dusty print on his glistening coat.

Jake and Marcus joined Ricki at Diablo's stall with smiles on their faces.

"That is definitely *your* horse. At least, your fingerprints are on him," Marcus said, laughing.

"He looks great," Jake said admiringly.

"Compared to me," grinned Ricki, and looked down at her clothes. "I wouldn't have thought that it was so difficult to groom a horse with one hand."

"Well," Marcus said, "you don't look any better when you use two hands!"

"Thanks, I didn't really need to know that!" Ricki grabbed her hoof tool and bent over with a groan, but Marcus stood there and pushed her aside.

"Wait, honey, that's impossible to do with one hand. Out of my way, I'll do it."

Ricki looked at her father with amazement. "You?" she asked, and glanced at Jake, who nodded yes.

"He can do it. He had a terrific teacher who taught him everything in a quick course!"

"*Quick* course? Jake made me clean out the hooves of 10 horses, one after the other, before he was satisfied and I felt clinically dead." Marcus was exaggerating, and then he bent over to do Diablo's hooves. A slight sheen of perspiration was on his forehead as Diablo jerked away. Marcus was still slightly skittish of these big animals.

"He cleaned out the hooves of two horses—Diablo and Frisbee—but considering, he does pretty well, don't you think?" Jake asked his young friend.

"If someone had told me a week ago that my father, *my father,* would even dare to go near a horse, I wouldn't have believed it!" Half amused yet with deep admiration, Ricki watched her father work. She had to admit it had taken her longer to get used to being near the hooves of horses than it had him.

"You should hold his leg up higher, that will make it easier," she said, while Marcus worked even harder.

"Yeah, I know. The only question is, does your horse know that!? He is leaning on me with his full weight."

Jake laughed as Diablo set his hoof lightly on the ground, just missing Marcus's foot. Startled, Ricki's father jumped aside and smashed into the wall of the stall.

"He just wants to see if he can play this game with you. Normally, he lets me do it with no problem," Ricki said with an air of self-satisfaction.

"A stupid game," declared Marcus, rubbing his bruised shoulder.

Diablo looked at him questioningly. Was his new friend giving up so quickly? After all, he had three other hooves that needed to be cleaned out.

"Give me the tool!" Jake took the scraper and ap-

14

proached the horse. "So, my boy! That's the end of the game. Lift that leg!"

Willingly, Diablo stepped to the side and lifted his hooves voluntarily, one after the other. The stable master could work without straining. When Jake had cleaned the last hoof, he patted the horse on the croup and said, "Okay, my boy, we're finished!" Then Diablo set his rear left hoof down carefully.

Marcus watched, fascinated. "Try to understand these animals!" He laughed and shook his head, while Ricki and Jake poked each other and grinned.

After a while, admiring her horse with pride, Ricki sighed deeply. "If only I could ride again," she said, and looked at her bandaged arm. "Finally, I have my own horse, and I can't even take care of him myself. That's really crappy!"

"Well, I don't think Diablo will blame you," Marcus said to his daughter as he stroked Diablo's back. "He'll probably enjoy resting before you start riding him day and night."

"Oh, Daddy, don't exaggerate so much. As if I would ever overwork him," Ricki protested, but the gleam in her eye betrayed the fact that she would probably spend every free minute with her horse, with a lot of time in the saddle. But she knew that it would be a few weeks before that could happen. "At least five weeks of rest for the arm," Dr. Evans had advised after examining the X-rays at the hospital. Shortly after the attack, Ricki had regretted that it was left arm, not her right, that was in a sling. Had it been her right, she could have avoided many tests and papers at school. But now she was glad to have at least one good arm.

She had decided to change her attitude about several things, particularly schoolwork. She was determined to do her homework right away and also to study for tests. If necessary, she would even take tutoring lessons in math, or at least take the extra lessons at school to catch up after last year's bad performance. She let schoolwork go much too much, but now it was clear that had to change. She had not received Diablo as a reward for her bad grades.

"For you I will get good grades," she whispered softly to her horse. "I promise. You'll have to let me make myself comfortable in a corner of your stall, so I can do my homework and still visit with you. Too bad you don't speak French. Otherwise you could help me learn new vocabulary words."

Diablo snorted and shook his beautiful, powerful head. *Vocabulary words—and French ones, to boot—that is a bit too much!*

Delighted, Ricki shook her head in imitation, her ponytail bobbing, then leaned happily against her horse. She didn't notice her father, who had been listening to her words, quietly walk away. He had heard her say that she wanted to work harder at school. He knew if Ricki really had decided to do that, then no one would be able to stop her from achieving more. Diablo really seemed to work miracles.

*

Around 11 a.m. Marcus reminded Ricki that it was time to leave.

"Ricki, it's time to go. We shouldn't make your mother wait with lunch on the very first day of your owning a horse."

Ricki made a grimace. Darn! The time had gone too quickly. When she realized that she would be sitting at home for the rest of the day while her wonderful horse was alone at the stable, it made her impatient.

"Oh, Daddy, can't we stay here? Just half an hour more? Or can I stay during lunch? You have to bring Jake back anyway."

"Oh, I almost forgot. Jake, Brigitte said we were to bring you with us for lunch."

The old stable master stopped forking hay into a now-vacant stall. He put down his pitchfork and walked, his head held to one side, joining Marcus and Ricki. "What? You want me to come for lunch?"

"Brigitte wants to make sure you have a good, hot home-cooked meal. She'll be furious if we don't bring you."

"But I was at your house just yesterday. Maybe you'd rather be without guests for a while, after all—"

"Nonsense, Mom cooks too much anyway, and besides, you're an honorary member of our family now!" Ricki interrupted him forcefully. "Harry is waiting for the next scary story from you. As far as I know, he's writing them all down in a notebook."

"What, that scamp is writing them down? Well, I'll put a stop to that! Next he'll be telling my stories to his friends!"

"You can bet on it," grinned Marcus. He had fetched Jake's old winter jacket out of the tack room and held it out to him.

"Come on, your horses can do without you for two hours, don't you agree?"

Jake gave up. He grumbled a bit while he put on his jacket, but Ricki and her father knew that he was glad to escape his loneliness and that he enjoyed being with them at their house.

Marcus held open the entrance door of the riding academy for Jake and his daughter, but Ricki remained where she stood. Pleadingly she looked at her father. "Please,

Daddy, don't be mad, but I just *can't* go home now! I am so happy, and after all, it's my first day with Diablo. If I can't ride him, then at least I want to be near him. Anyway, I'm not hungry at all, and—"

Marcus was undecided. "But your mother—"

"Well, maybe if I eat a portion for Ricki it will appease her. Don't you think?" Jake quickly intervened. He completely understood what Ricki was feeling. She just couldn't leave her horse now. She needed to be near him, see him, hear him, and feel him. She wanted to bond with him. Even a good lunch prepared by her mother couldn't compare to the first day of owning a horse.

Jake understood how important it was for Ricki to be alone with her horse for a while. Some people probably thought he was a recluse and an odd fellow, but when it came to riding and horses, he knew everything. No one could handle the horses the way he could. He was with them every day and knew how they felt.

He knew Ricki needed to get to know Diablo, and it was equally important that Diablo become accustomed to his new owner. He knew, too, that the treatment of his former owner, Frank Cooper, had made a damaging impression on the horse and, as a consequence, Ricki would be confronted with these difficulties when she began to ride Diablo. Cooper had made Diablo even more afraid of jumping by hitting him, so when the horse saw the whip he panicked— he had felt the impact of one often enough. These were all things Ricki knew only a little bit about. They could be overcome only by Ricki's gaining the horse's trust and confidence.

"Marcus, if Diablo is to learn to trust people again and become a good mount, he has to get used to having Ricki around," explained Jake.

Marcus shrugged. "Okay, I'll allow it. You are lucky to have Jake on your side."

"I know," laughed Ricki happily.

"If you should get hungry, go up to my apartment. I have some cheese and salami in the fridge, and there's a loaf of bread on the kitchen table," Jake yelled to Ricki as the two men got into the car.

Ricki waved to show that she had understood. Actually, she wanted to wait until the car had disappeared from her sight, but she decided to return to the warm stall right away. It was getting much colder outside.

Ricki started down the corridor, then stopped for a moment. She listened to the familiar noises of the animals, their chewing, the shuffling of their hooves, the snorting and the whinnies of these wonderful creatures, and all of a sudden she realized that she could never give up these moments in her life. Having fallen in love with horses, she knew she couldn't live without them ever again.

Happier than she had ever been, Ricki held back her tears of joy before she ran back to her horse's stall, her heart beating wildly.

Her horse! She could hardly believe it; it still seemed like a dream. She entered the stall quietly and closed the door behind her. Slowly she sat down on the straw in the corner and looked at Diablo, who kept right on eating despite her presence. Why shouldn't he? He knew he had nothing to fear from Ricki.

As she watched him, she wondered again what Lark and Cathy would say when they found out she was now a horse owner. Would they be jealous...envious? Probably not. Afterall, they were her two best friends.

I was pretty mean to them, Ricki acknowledged to herself, remembering their last conversation shortly before

19

Christmas. She had let out her frustration over the stable ban on her two friends, so the three of them had not parted on the best of terms. She had to apologize for sure. While she was trying to decide what she would say to the girls, her eyelids began to close, and soon there was light, regular snoring to be heard, in addition to the snorting of the horses. Ricki had fallen asleep.

*

She felt almost weightless on the back of her horse, galloping away. Diablo's legs became more and more forceful, and with every stride he seemed to spring higher and wider. The freshly fallen snow welled up like clouds around his hooves, creating a wall behind them that made it impossible to turn back. Ricki felt the first rays of sun break through the snowstorm and shine in her face, warming her.

Diablo shook his head impatiently, and Ricki loosened the reins. Unhindered, the wonderful black horse stretched himself and raced through the wide, white winter landscape. He kept running and running until he was far from his past and his problems, then slowly he reduced his pace. He had left the dark snow clouds behind him, and now he was standing in a sunny, lush green forest glade.

In her dream, Ricki dismounted Diablo. She undid the saddle girth and the bit. She trusted the black horse completely and knew he wouldn't disappoint her.

Diablo sensed his freedom and felt the desire to run away, but the invisible thread binding him and Ricki together was so strong that all he did was trot happily around the girl. She turned her face to him and slowly walked around in a circle as well. She was so happy when Diablo suddenly came to her and, with a loud and happy whinny, reared up on his hind legs directly in front of her.

She stopped and stood still, without fear, because she knew Diablo just wanted to thank her for the friendship, love, and affection she had shown him. Once again, Diablo reared up almost vertically into the air, challenging Ricki to enjoy her freedom with him as well. And so the girl jumped on his back without a saddle, and they galloped away together toward their happiness.

Chapter 2

The chill of the stable disturbed Ricki's sleep. Lost in her dream, she became fitful, restless; she tossed and turned. The rustling of the straw and the dull ache in her left shoulder awakened her, and she opened her eyes. For a moment, she was completely disoriented—she had *no* idea where she was—but Diablo's warm breath in her hair led her quickly back to reality.

Carefully she raised her good arm and pulled Diablo's head down by the halter strap until she could press her forehead against his. They stayed liked that for a few seconds, then Diablo jerked his head back and looked nervously over the stall along the corridor with his ears pointed forward.

Ricki got up feeling a little stiff, but after a few stretches she felt like her old self again. Gradually her dream came back to her, detail by detail.

She was riding Diablo, and she had had an indescribable feeling: She'd never felt as safe on any other horse, or as close to any other animal, as she did while galloping breathlessly across the meadow astride her Diablo.

"It's too bad, my darling little devil, it was just a dream. But we'll do it some time; that's for sure—when I'm back to normal," she said as she scratched Diablo behind the ears.

The black horse was still staring fixedly down the corridor. Ricki—who had grown curious—followed his gaze, but all she could see was Lupo, the little stray tomcat who frequented the stalls, running around the corner of the tack room. She giggled softly. "Don't tell me you don't know him? He's been in the stalls longer than both of us together," she said. Diablo searched about for a little bundle of hay that might have fallen out of the rack, but it was obvious that he'd already eaten everything in his stall that was edible.

"Man, you really eat a lot." Ricki left the stall to look for the carrots she thought were still in her grooming basket. As she was going past the sliding door leading to the riding hall, the thought struck her that maybe she could—

Determined, she turned and ran back to her horse, who was looking at her as if to say, *What? No carrot?* Ricki grinned as she opened the stall door and took hold of Diablo's halter.

"Come here, my little devil. We're going to move around a bit. That will do us both good."

Diablo seemed unconvinced, and the closer they got to the entrance door to the riding hall, the slower he moved. Finally, he stopped. Ricki pulled and pulled on his halter but she couldn't budge him—Diablo wasn't moving an inch.

Ricki talked to him with the patience of an angel, but her horse remained stubborn. His eyes filled with fear, and he began to shake all over.

"What's wrong, boy?" asked Ricki quietly while she patted him on the neck to comfort him. "Did Lupo scare you? That can't be it, can it? He's much smaller than you are! You know what? Let's just go inside, and then you can do whatever you like. Won't that be great? To be able to do

23

whatever you want? You can stand still, run around, roll around, wow, Diablo, that would really be something! When was the last time you could just move around and do anything you wanted? Cooper probably never let you do anything; all he ever did was hit you and mistreat you with spurs and whip—but that's all over."

While Ricki was trying to calm her horse with words, she suddenly realized what was wrong.

"Gosh—I'm an idiot!" she declared, and slapped her palm against her forehead. "Diablo, your owner is really stupid!" Saying that, she turned the black horse in the corridor so that he was facing in the opposite direction. Now he was willing to go with her, and as she entered the riding hall through the main entrance, he was right beside her.

"Why didn't I think of that right away?" she mumbled, shaking her head.

Frank Cooper had always led Diablo to the ring through the sliding door, and the horse associated this entrance with the pain inflicted on him afterward by Cooper's mistreatment.

Ricki now understood that it would take some time before Diablo could enter the ring through that door without fear.

Once in the riding ring, she let him go, and closed the railing as fast as she could with just one arm. Diablo followed her and stood directly behind her as she turned around.

"What's wrong? Don't you want to play?" Ricki walked to the middle of the ring, and Diablo followed her submissively. He seemed unaware that he was free.

At first Ricki thought it was wonderful that Diablo followed her. But she also understood that it was important for him to know that he had the freedom to run about wherever he wanted to. But this was a completely new concept for Diablo, who never had been allowed to move unrestrainedly while under Cooper's ownership. Unsure what to do, he remained standing, while Ricki waved her arms in front of his nose and tried to get him to run. He didn't seem to understand what she wanted, and stared at her in puzzlement.

"Run, my darling! You have the whole ring to yourself, and no one will punish you for running away. Do you hear that? Go! Jump! Go on, little devil, enjoy your freedom."

Ricki walked backward slowly toward the railing door, waving her arms wildly. Maybe she just needed to give Diablo some space, so that he could feel freer. But the horse seemed to be of a completely different opinion. He wouldn't stop following her and there was no doubt that he would not let her leave the riding hall alone. At first, Ricki thought about getting a guide whip, just to get Diablo going a bit, but then she remembered that Frank Cooper had taught the horse to fear the whip and so she quickly discarded the idea.

While she was observing her horse, who was trying to do everything perfectly so as not to make his owner angry, Lupo jumped from the gallery onto the railing with a mighty leap, making a hollow sound as he landed on the wooden railing right in front of Diablo. Ricki couldn't decide who was more frightened: the tomcat; Diablo; or she, herself.

Lupo ducked down, lay his ears flat on his head, and hissed loudly. Diablo jerked as though struck by lightning, and shook all through his gleaming body. Then he turned on his rear legs and galloped off in escape. He seemed to have awoken from his "sleeping-beauty" trance and now raced across the dirt floor, sending the sand flying in all di-

25

rections. Ricki ran back to the middle of the floor in order to observe her horse safely.

Over and over again, Diablo raced back and forth across the ring. There were many times Ricki was afraid he wouldn't be able to stop in time and that he'd break right through the railing.

Diablo kept it up for about 15 minutes, then he began to trot. He held his head arched high and his tail aloft, and walked with the bearing of a show horse. His hooves seemed to hang suspended in the air for a second before setting down on the ground.

Ricki couldn't get enough of him. Only now did she begin to appreciate how wonderful Diablo was and what a truly special and loving present she had received. Yet, she still couldn't quite believe it. At that moment, Diablo came toward her and reared up on his hind legs, just as he had done in her dream.

He seemed to be saying, *Look at me! Here I am—I am big—I am strong, and you will always be able to depend on me!*

Ricki felt what Diablo wanted to say to her. When his hooves were down on the ground again, she ran to him and put her arm around his neck. Happy, she buried her face in his mane, while Diablo stood completely still. It was a picture of trust, a magical moment, and Lark and Cathy saw it as well. They had been standing in the gallery staring over the railing into the riding hall, transfixed.

"What is she doing?" whispered Lark. Cathy, stunned by what she had just witnessed, yelled to her friend, "Ricki, what in the world are you doing?"

Diablo jerked in surprise as he heard the loud unfamiliar voice calling. Ricki turned around. "Cathy—Lark—what are you guys doing at the stable now? Did your parents throw you out because you hated your Christmas presents?"

"She's got a sense of humor!" Lark shook her head. "Hey, what in the world are you doing here? I thought you were in bed resting your broken bones. And I thought you weren't allowed to go to the stable. Or did some good fairy change your C's and D's into A's and B's?"

Ricki grinned. "That would have been terrific, but it wasn't quite that easy."

Diablo nudged her in the back. *Tell the truth!* he seemed to say.

"Well," Ricki admitted, "if you take out the bad grades, the rest wasn't really that difficult. By the way, our family just got bigger!"

"What?" Cathy couldn't believe her ears. "Your mother's pregnant?"

Ricki laughed. "I'll explain it all to you later. But first, Diablo needs to run for a while longer."

As though he had understood her words, the black horse turned aside from his owner and trotted a few steps away. But soon he was standing behind Ricki again. Perhaps, he'd had enough for today and longed for the peace and quiet of his stall.

Ricki reached for his halter and led him out of the riding ring. Cathy and Lark followed a respectful distance behind. They didn't know what to think of their friend's behavior, but they were in agreement over this one thing: They would never take someone's horse out of the stall without asking first, even if it was their favorite horse.

Ricki tied up Diablo in the corridor and fed him her last three carrots. Then she brushed his sweaty coat until it gleamed once again. Cathy and Lark watched her without saying a word. But when Ricki asked them to

27

help her with scraping out the hooves, Lark cleared her throat.

"Ah, hmmm, … well, I'll help you, but—"

"Do you think what you're doing is right?" Cathy finished Lark's sentence, a little distantly. "You know, I don't think the new owner will like what you're doing."

Ricki grinned. "Oh, I'm sure that it will please him—that is, her. I think she'll be delighted that you are helping me."

Cathy shook her head, perplexed, and Lark reached for the scraper. "Well, if you think so—"

Cautiously, Lark approached Diablo's hooves.

"You can go right up to him. He won't hurt you. Right, little devil? You're just glad your hooves are clean again."

Ricki stroked her horse lovingly, while Lark began to work on the hooves. Diablo stood perfectly still, like he was supposed to, and later was glad to be brought back to his stall and rubbed and stroked affectionately by the girls.

"C'mon, tell us what's going on. A new family member?" Curious, Cathy looked at Ricki, who had just pulled Diablo's head down to her.

"May I introduce you? This is Diablo Sulai, Ricki Sulai's horse since December twenty-fourth of this year!"

"You're joking, right?" asked Cathy in disbelief.

"I think Ricki's concussion has left a permanent injury. Now she thinks she has her own horse!" Lark couldn't decide whether she was angry or amused. She thought her friend was making fun of her.

"You two don't believe me? Ask Jake. He gave me the horse for Christmas."

"What nonsense! So the stable master gave you the horse as a present! Your imagination is really running away

28

with you. Next, you'll tell us that your father has learned to ride!"

Ricki thought that over for a second. "No, he can't ride yet, but he does know how to muck out the stall and groom horses."

Lark rolled her eyes. "This is just too weird! I can't take it anymore. Cathy, are you coming? We wanted to sign up for the riding schedule."

Cathy was standing, undecided, in front of Diablo's stall.

"You guys still don't believe me?" asked Ricki, disappointed that her best friends weren't taking her seriously.

"No, I just don't believe it." Lark turned around haughtily and was about to leave when Ricki said softly, "Hey, you guys...what I wanted to tell you...our last talk...you know...I was really horrible. I'm sorry...really!"

Lark turned back to Ricki and grinned. "What, are you apologizing?"

Ricki nodded sadly. "It won't happen again. I was just in such a bad mood. Everything—my grades, my parents, the sale of Diablo."

"... and the dumb chitchat of your two best friends!" Now Cathy laughed, too. "So, let's forget about it! We're not always in the best mood either."

"Especially when Ricki is trying to make us believe that she got a horse as a reward for her bad grades."

"I didn't say as a reward, but—"

"C'mon, stop it! Enough already!" Lark seemed really ticked off. "This just isn't a laughing matter!"

Cathy hesitated. Was Lark right? She couldn't decide whether to believe Ricki or not. Finally, she decided to follow Lark's lead and pay no attention to Ricki. Maybe Ricki was still suffering from the aftereffects of Cooper's attack. It was probably better just to ignore her.

29

Ricki shrugged. Her girlfriends refused to believe her, and she was beginning to feel almost embarrassed about owning her own horse.

"Then don't believe me," she said softly and left Diablo's stall. Sitting on the bench in the corridor with her grooming basket, she watched silently as Lark and Cathy talked to their favorite horses more loudly than usual.

A short time later, Marcus and Jake returned. As they approached, Jake, patting his stomach, remarked, "Good grief, I am so full, you could roll me alongside the feed cart today. Brigitte is really a good cook!"

Marcus grinned at Ricki. "Don't smile too soon, Ricki. Jake couldn't eat everything. That means that your mother insists that you come home now and eat something. After all, you have to get your strength back if you want to ride your horse!" Then, "Oh, Lark and Cathy are here already!" he said, just noticing Ricki's friends at a nearby stall. "I should have known! You girls are no better than my daughter. Hello, you two!"

Neither of them could reply. They stared at Ricki's father with their mouths open. Had they heard right? Had he just said "*your* horse" to Ricki?

Ricki got up, said good-bye to Jake, and gave the two girls a somewhat sad look. Then she and her father left the stall. She had the impression that her friendship with the two girls wouldn't be the same as it was before Diablo belonged to her. But she hoped she was wrong.

Wide-eyed, Lark and Cathy watched her leave.

"I can't believe it! This is too weird! Ricki has a horse and didn't tell us."

"Yes, she did."

"Only today. If that had happened to me, I would have called you immediately."

"But, Lark, she only got him yesterday, and we didn't believe her today when she told us!"

"I still don't believe it!" Full of envy and doubt, Lark stared out the window.

"Hey, you two, you have to get used to it! Diablo belongs to Ricki now, and that's good. But just so you can get your heads straight, you can help me!" Jake grabbed two pitchforks and gave one to each of the girls.

"Mix the straw and the hay together, please—as fast as you can. I stayed at lunch too long, and now the horses are hungry."

Lark and Cathy were still not sure what was going on, but they didn't have time to worry about it. Jake gave them plenty to do. But as Cathy came by Diablo's stall, she stopped for a moment.

"Hello, you. Do you have any idea how much I envy Ricki having you?"

Jake, who was standing behind her said, "Envy is a weed in the garden of friendship!" which made Cathy feel bad about what she had said.

She decided to visit Ricki as soon as possible. Friends are supposed to be glad for each other when they are happy, not envious and spiteful. It would be great to have a friend who had her own horse. Cathy hoped she would be able to ride Diablo some times. After all, it could take quite a while until Ricki was able to ride again.

Chapter 3

Against all expectations, Marcus drove his daughter to the stable every day during vacation. However, he did have one condition: He would not drive her there early in the morning but sometime in the afternoon. He wanted to be able to sleep late during his well-earned Christmas vacation.

Ricki agreed. For her, the important thing was seeing Diablo; it didn't matter what time. She could hardly wait until she didn't have to rely on her parents and could get to the stable on her own. But that seemed like forever.

When Marcus had to go back to work, Brigitte offered to drive her daughter to the stables. Sometimes Harry went with them, so he could be part of it, too.

Harry, whom Ricki always referred to as a pain in the neck, turned out to be a real asset in the stall. He enjoyed helping everyone, holding the horses by the reins, getting the bits. As a reward, the owners allowed him to mount their horses for a moment, and he winked at his sister proudly from atop the horses' backs.

"Hey, Ricki, look where I am!"

Ricki just rolled her eyes, but secretly she was very pleased, because she knew that her love affair with horses had begun in exactly the same way.

*

It wasn't long before everyone in the riding club had heard that Ricki was Diablo's new owner. Most of her riding colleagues were happy for her, but some were mean. Many of them owned horses themselves—and they shook their heads in bewilderment and declared Jake to be even crazier than they'd thought. The stable master just laughed when he heard someone say he could have made a bundle if he had sold Diablo instead of giving him away.

"I've become richer than you think," he usually answered. "Being rich doesn't always have to do with what's in your wallet, it has to do with what's in your heart!" After all, it was through Diablo that he had found a home in the Sulai family and a good friend in Ricki's father. This was much more important to him than a few thousand dollars in the bank. And he knew that Diablo was in good hands with Ricki, and that was the most important thing in the world to him.

In spite of her injury, Ricki came to the stable every day. Jake was amazed that she was able to take on some of his work as well, even though she was still somewhat handicapped. He knew she was supposed to take it easy, but every time he was out of sight, Ricki began working on the stalls or feeding the horses, although a bit awkwardly.

Ricki just wouldn't let herself slow down; she was so happy that Jake had given her her dream horse. And, over time, she was beginning to feel much better as long as she didn't make any sudden movements, which still caused a lot of pain in her shoulder and reminded her that the broken collarbone had not healed yet.

Ricki and Cathy were still very good friends, but Lark had distanced herself from Ricki. She was jealous of her and her horse and now sided with those who ignored Ricki and Diablo completely.

"How can she behave like that?" Cathy wondered aloud, shaking her head as Lark walked stiffly past Diablo's stall without greeting them. Lark had decided to ignore Cathy too, as long as she was friends with Ricki. Cathy hadn't told Ricki that she'd had a big fight with Lark.

"She's as arrogant as all the other horse owners," said Lark nastily during the break between French and geography. "She thinks she's better than us! Cathy, don't you see that she doesn't care about us? She treats us like dirt—and you play up to her and act like nothing's wrong!"

"Nonsense!" Cathy's cheeks turned red as she saw that all her classmates were listening to what Lark said.

"Not nonsense," Lark snapped, her eyes blazing with envy and anger. "Don't you get it? You don't have anything to show for following after Ricki. Has she asked you, even once, if you'd like to ride Diablo? No, she hasn't! And you'll see, she won't ask you! She's just as bad as the rest! If I had a horse, you could ride him every day, that I promise you!"

Cathy was almost ashamed for Lark's outburst. But to be honest, she'd have to admit that it did hurt her a little that all she was allowed to do was help Ricki scrape out Diablo's hooves. Ricki never offered to let her ride.

"Maybe I'll never ride Diablo, but that doesn't mean Ricki is a jerk," Cathy said, trying tried to defend her friend. But Lark wouldn't be stopped.

"How would you describe someone who won't let her best friends ride her horse? Haven't you noticed that she only talks with Kevin now? It's Kevin this, Kevin that—she doesn't even care about us anymore!"

Cathy was glad when the last-period bell finally rang, and she didn't have to listen to any more accusations about Ricki. She hated this kind of talk, but Lark had managed to plant the seeds of uncertainty in Cathy's heart. Was it possible that Ricki didn't care about their friendship any longer? Was she just using Cathy to help care for her horse while she was still unable to do it all? And, as far as Kevin was concerned, he was more than just nice; Cathy had butterflies in her stomach every time she talked with him. Ricki's growing friendship with Kevin was actually more of a reason for Cathy to be jealous of Ricki than her ownership of Diablo. There were days when she had to ask herself how Ricki ended up with a horse *and* Kevin as boyfriend. Up to now, however, she had managed to be fair to Ricki, although Lark did her best to damage their friendship. It almost seemed as though there had never been a true friendship between Lark and Ricki.

Naturally Ricki was very sad that things turned out as they had, but Jake comforted her. He explained that real friendship was often tested in situations like this—when fortune smiled on one friend and not the other—which made Ricki believe that maybe she had been wrong all along, thinking Lark was her friend.

*

The vacation went by quickly—as all school vacations do—and soon classes resumed.

Ricki was treated like a heroine after Kevin and Cathy explained to everyone how she had intervened when Diablo had been mistreated. Their classmates' admiration of Ricki made Lark even more jealous and, in the following weeks, she was able to convince some of her school chums that Ricki's new status as a horse owner showed her up as the snob she really was.

Now the class was divided into two groups. On Ricki's side were Kevin and Cathy, those students who loved animals and admired her courage, and those who were genuinely happy the events of the previous weeks ended in good fortune for both Ricki and Diablo. Lark had the others on her side, and hung out with classmates she previously didn't like at all.

In spite of Lark's negative attitude, Ricki was happy. She had Diablo, and therefore she was willing to give up other things, even her longtime friendship with Lark. Besides, she was convinced Lark would come around.

*

Today was the big day.

Ricki had just had her last examination at the hospital, and Dr. Evans had finally given her the okay to begin riding again.

"So, my girl," he said, smiling. "That's it! Your collarbone is almost as good as new, but that doesn't mean you should fall on it again. It will take a little while until it is completely healed. So please—no more fistfights with horse owners!"

Ricki laughed. "I think I can do without that for a while," she said. Then she waved happily and hurried out of the examining room. When she got outside, Cathy was waiting for her with their bikes. They jumped on and rode quickly to the stable.

"You know what? Jake talked Doctor Hofer into giving him an old saddle," Ricki said, almost out of breath from pedaling so fast.

"What? Our vet has old saddles just lying around?"

"No, but he just bought a new dressage saddle, and Jake told him that since he has only one backside, he needs only one saddle!"

Cathy almost fell off her bike, she was laughing so hard. "That's typical of him. He's getting more and more outrageous!"

"No way," said Ricki. "Jake is always respectful. But when I think of how much a new saddle costs, I am really glad that the vet has only one backside."

"And now you really want to try it out, don't you?" Cathy asked. Ricki's eyes began to glisten.

"Of course, what kind of a question is that? I have waited *sooo* long for this moment. I can't wait to see how Diablo reacts to a rider."

"Be careful, you know … your shoulder," Cathy warned her.

But Ricki just laughed. "Thanks, Mommy! It'll be okay!"

*

Diablo sensed the inner unrest in Ricki as she fastened the saddle and the bit with shaking hands.

"Gee—I'm so excited! It's as though today was the first time I ever mounted a horse," she mumbled softly to herself. Jake, who was as nervous as she was, watched her from the corridor.

"You don't have to be scared," he said with forced calm. "Diablo just has to forget Cooper and the way he rode. That man beat and kicked him, but Diablo will notice quickly that you won't hurt him. And when he knows that, then you will have the best horse in the world!"

Ricki nodded. "I'm not scared," but her voice didn't sound as convincing as her words. Inwardly, she scolded herself for being a coward. After all, she had waited so long for this moment. In the last weeks there hadn't been a single day when she hadn't looked after Diablo, and there had never been a minute when she thought anything could go wrong when she finally got to ride him. But today—

"Put your heart into the saddle before you mount," she heard Jake say. She took a deep breath, patted Diablo on the neck, and then she held the reins tightly in her hand.

"Well, here goes," she said, and Jake opened the stall door.

"You're doing fine," he told her. More excited than ever, she led Diablo down the corridor.

Cathy was already waiting for her at the ring in order to open the railing door. Time seemed to stand still for Ricki and Diablo.

While Cathy and Jake quietly found seats in the gallery, Ricki led her horse all across the riding ring with long reins. Every once in a while she stopped to tighten the girth. She didn't want to do anything too hastily.

Diablo nudged her gently in the back, as though to tell her: *Hey, what's the matter? I'm ready.*

Ricki glanced once more to the gallery and then led her horse to the center of the ring. She tested the girth once more, took the reins in one hand, and put her foot in the stirrup.

She pulled herself up powerfully and then cautiously eased herself down on the saddle. She spoke gently to Diablo the whole time, but neither Cathy nor Jake could hear what she was saying. Diablo's ears turned back and forth while he listened to the words being spoken right behind his head. He loved the sound of Ricki's voice; it gave him a feeling of absolute security.

"So, that's good, sweetie. I think the worst is behind us.

I'm in the saddle—that wasn't so bad, was it? I don't have any spurs or whips with me. We don't need that stuff. So, let's try our luck. Forward…"

The black horse began to move. Ricki, who hadn't sat in a saddle for weeks, felt a little unsure of herself, but after a few minutes, she found her old rhythm and forgot about her fears.

It was wonderful to ride Diablo. He had a wide step and didn't need to be urged. After two turns around the ring, he got used to the reins and was able to maintain a perfect posture, even after Ricki started to trot and then gallop.

He reacted to the lightest gestures from Ricki, which were invisible to the onlookers. Diablo seemed to know in advance what Ricki wanted him to do, and her ride was almost perfect. As she often did, Ricki looked into the big mirror on the wall, and her heart leapt. There she was—the girl with the most wonderful horse in the world underneath her saddle!

She had never felt this happy before while riding. Spontaneously she loosened the reins and bent down over his neck. As she hugged him lovingly, tears of joy fell onto his mane.

Jake and Cathy saw Ricki bent over and heard her sniffling. They jumped up, afraid she was hurt.

"Ricki? Is everything okay?" yelled Jake from the gallery.

Ricki sat back up and waved happily. "I'm just so happy," she said, laughing and crying at the same time. "This is the most wonderful horse I have ever ridden!"

"No wonder," replied Jake, grinning with relief. "It's your horse!"

After a good half-hour, Ricki gave up the reins and

39

sprang out of the saddle. She loosened the girth and led Diablo away to dry him off, stopping frequently just to give her horse a hug. "Incredible. Absolutely fabulous. Fantastic." She couldn't calm down, she was so hyper with happiness.

Diablo, on the other hand, seemed very relaxed. This was the first time he hadn't been mistreated after a ride in the indoor ring.

Happily, Ricki led the horse back to the stall, where Jake, beaming, awaited them.

"I knew you wouldn't disappoint me," he said as he scratched the horse lovingly under his mane. His voice had an unfamiliar, but attractive, youthful quality to it.

Cathy's eyes were shining too. She had to admit that she was a little disappointed at first that Ricki hadn't invited her to take a ride on Diablo. But she soon realized that this being the first time out for both owner and horse after their injuries, Ricki very sensibly hadn't wanted to overdo it; nor did she want to risk overworking her horse. Anyway, it was only right that the first ride on her dream horse belonged to Ricki.

"Did you guys see the gaits? The trot? The gallop? I don't understand why Cooper couldn't appreciate what an intelligent, sensitive, and responsive animal this horse is; he'd react to the touch of a mosquito's wing! One thing I know for sure: I'm going to hide my whip in the darkest corner of the attic. I never liked to use it anyway."

She praised Diablo without a pause. "And when I mounted, he stood completely still. Every motion he makes is effortless. You have the feeling he wants to perform and please."

"Then you two have something in common!" Lark said coldly, striding past them with an arrogant expression on her face.

Ricki had never heard her formerly chipper friend sound so frosty.

"She's jealous, but never mind, she'll get over it!" Jake said easily.

Ricki turned back to her horse. She brushed his sweaty coat with enthusiasm until it was smooth and cleaned his hooves before she put him back into the stall. She would have liked to stay with him, but she decided to go home to study for tomorrow's lessons. She didn't want to disappoint the people who were responsible for her great happiness by getting bad grades again.

"But tomorrow I'll bring all my school stuff with me to the stable. We'll see how you do with French and biology." Laughing, she gave her horse a kiss on the nose, although he would much rather have had a carrot. Then, saying her good-byes to Jake and Cathy, she picked up her grooming basket and practically skipped down the corridor to the exit.

Cathy watched her go with a puzzled shake of her head. "What's happened to her? Is she sick? Or did she get carbon-dioxide poisoning while she was riding? I've never seen her act so nutsy!"

"She's probably healthier than she's ever been. She finally understands what's important for her," Jake smiled, then turned and walked slowly toward the tack room.

Cathy watched Jake walking away. "Boy, everyone is acting so weird lately," she mumbled. Shrugging her shoulders, she turned back to collect her backpack and jacket. She didn't see Jake grab at his chest, groaning, and, suddenly changing his direction, stumble out of the stable toward his apartment.

*

41

The next day, Ricki appeared earlier than usual at the stalls. She threw her school bag carelessly onto the bench under the riding schedule and ran, armed with her basket of grooming tools, straight to Diablo, who was already greeting her loudly.

"Hello, little devil. How are you? Wait, I brought you a treat."

Excited, she searched her pockets for the new equine treats she had bought on her way home from school. "Cookies with apple flavor! Let's see how you like that," she said, holding a few out to him in the palm of her hand. While Diablo was chewing with gusto, she sniffed at the bag of remaining large cookies.

"Hmm, it really does smell like apple," she said, and bit off a little piece. She made a face. "Well, I like steak better. Amazing what they give horses to eat."

Diablo didn't seem to think the cookies were that bad. He loved to eat and began looking for more treats in Ricki's pockets.

"Wait, wait! You'll get the rest later!" Ricki put the bag of treats out of reach and started to groom her horse. She was pleased to see that there were no remaining scars from Cooper's mistreatment in Diablo's coat. He looked wonderful. "So, it's true," she told him. "Time heals all wounds. Well, at least the visible ones. The ones in the heart will always remain just a little bit. What do you think?"

Ricki saddled her horse and led him, this time without fear, into the riding ring. She enjoyed a wonderful ride for almost an hour. Diablo responded to her gestures even more sensitively than he had the day before.

Later, she sat in a corner of his stall satisfied and happy. Diablo eyes were closed and he was half-asleep. It appeared he enjoyed the ride also.

He probably has as many sore muscles as I do, she thought, as she opened her French vocabulary book.

"Let's begin," she mumbled softly to herself, so as not to wake Diablo.

The paper rustled quietly as she wrote out her vocabulary words. She glanced at her horse, but he wasn't disturbed at all and didn't even flinch.

"You are wonderful," she whispered with a last intense look at Diablo. Then she concentrated on her homework.

*

Jake was a little paler than usual as he fed the horses in the afternoon. But Ricki was so happy with Diablo that she didn't even notice. She was a little surprised, though, that he stopped so often to rest as he pushed the feed cart along the corridor.

"Do you have sore muscles, too?" she teased him, but unlike other days, he didn't laugh at her joke.

He stopped to rest again and tried to take a deep breath. "Oh my, I just can't seem to get my breath today."

"You shouldn't smoke so much, Jake," Ricki answered jovially. But she shoved him aside, and pushed the cart with youthful energy herself. "Take a break—I'll do it," she called over her shoulder. The old man nodded thankfully. He was worried about his problem breathing, plus the piercing pain in his chest, which kept coming back since last evening.

With one hand braced against the corridor wall, he slowly lowered himself down onto the bench and sat looking at Ricki, who was lovingly giving out the oats to the horses.

Thank God, Diablo is in good hands with her, he thought, a little sad. He had come to realize that, if his

43

health kept getting worse, his time as stable master would be shorter than he had anticipated.

He closed his eyes for a moment. *Just five minutes,* he thought. *Five minutes of sleep, then I'll continue.* Jake's chin fell onto his chest. When Ricki returned with the cart Jake was making a light grunting-snoring sound. She smiled. "Dear Jake, just sleep, and don't worry about anything. Your horses will be cared for as well as ever." Ricki grabbed the pitchfork and the cart and began to muck out the stalls, one after the other. She spread the straw in the stalls before she put the hay in the racks.

Strange, that no one else is in the stable, she thought, before she realized that today was the day off that Jake had fought so hard for.

Two and a half hours later, as Ricki was sweeping the corridor, Jake finally woke up. He had slept soundly and now he felt strong enough to do his work.

"Amazing, what five minutes of sleep can do," he said contentedly, and smiled at Ricki, who laughed out loud.

"Five minutes? But don't worry about it. Now you can quit for the day!"

Jake looked at her slightly confused, and then checked his watch.

"That isn't possible!" he groaned as Ricki replaced the broom. "Girl, I owe you," he said softly.

Ricki shook her head and clasped his hand to her heart. "No—no, Jake! You don't owe me, I owe you—and big time!"

Chapter 4

Ricki kept the same schedule in the days that followed. She had figured out a way to plan her free time so that neither schoolwork nor Diablo got short-changed.

She usually got home about 2:30 p.m., and liked having both her mother and Harry there. They had gotten used to sitting together enjoying an after-school snack and talking about everything and anything. That was exactly what Ricki had missed all those years before ... peacefully talking with the rest of the family.

Brigitte Sulai enjoyed these talks too. Although she thought she would miss going to work, that only lasted for the first few days of being at home. She had begun to use her free time to create beautiful watercolor landscapes after attending a painting course at night school.

"You really have talent, Mom," Ricki said again and again, and she meant it. When she thought about her own drawings, which looked like they were done by a kindergartner, she really had to admire her mother's gift.

Harry mostly fidgeted in his chair during these talks, impatient to get back in front of the TV. The only topic that seemed to interest him was what programs he would be allowed to watch.

But Brigitte and Ricki were happy that they could talk to

one another again. They were becoming more like friends than mother and daughter, which made their relationship much more satisfying.

After this daily family hour, Ricki usually got a start on her homework; after that, she went to the stable, no matter what the weather was like. Ricki spent at least an hour every day grooming and riding Diablo. She felt with every minute they spent together, they grew closer.

When the ride was over and Diablo was taken care of, Ricki sat down in the stall to continue with her homework. Studying with Diablo was really fun, but Ricki knew she had a lot of catching up to do. Schoolwork had been unimportant to her for too long, and she had a lot of difficulty with math. Even Diablo's presence and sympathetic looks couldn't help her there.

"Don't you know someone who could help you?" Jake asked one day as he looked over her shoulder. But he couldn't make any more sense out of the tables and diagrams in Ricki's textbook than she could. Although he felt better in general, Jake was still experiencing weakness in his legs, a fact he kept to himself and tried not to let get in the way of his chores.

"Hmm," considered Ricki. "Cathy is good at math, but she's been in such a bad mood the last few days. Maybe because she's been hanging out with Lark more often recently."

"Maybe it's because you haven't offered to let her ride," Jake suggested cautiously.

"What? Do you think so?"

The stable master nodded thoughtfully.

"Oh, man, if that's the reason … Do you think I should let her, Jake? But I'm not sure I want to. I don't want Diablo to start—"

"I understand you, you don't have to go on." Jake put his hand on her shoulder. "Now that you are responsible for the horse, you can be sure that he is well treated only when you take care of him yourself. Is that it?"

Ricki contritely lowered her eyes.

"But, you know, I think there'd be no problem if you let Cathy ride him every once in a while. You've seen the way she treats Holli. There's no difference between the care she gives Lillian's horse and the care you give Diablo."

"But Diablo is not Doc Holliday! He's much more sensitive than Lillian's horse. And anyway, if I let Cathy ride him now, it will look as though I let her ride only to get her to help me with math. And I don't want that either." Ricki was torn with conflict. The idea that someone else should ride her horse didn't appeal to her at all, even if it was her best friend.

"You shouldn't look at it like that," Jake advised. "Friends help out friends. But in the end, you have to make the decision. And I have no doubt that you will make the right one. If I didn't, then I wouldn't have given Diablo to you in the first place." Jake patted her shoulder again and then walked slowly away.

Ricki remained alone with Diablo, her thoughts, and her math book with all its perplexing problems. She tried to concentrate on the math problems but she kept thinking about Cathy. Of course she understood her friend's longing. Until only recently, they both had watched the horse owners with a shared desire, always hoping they would be invited to ride the owners' horses for a few minutes. Now Ricki was an owner, and it was only natural that, as Ricki's best friend, Cathy wished she would be asked if she wanted to ride Diablo. But Ricki was not yet ready to let others ride her horse.

Diablo stretched his beautiful head toward her, and Ricki embraced him lovingly.

"Okay, baby, let's not let any one else ride you just yet. Maybe later, but not right now. We're just getting used to one another." After a short hesitation, she added, "At the very worst, I will have one less friend, but I will have you to make up for it! You and Jake. And you two are much more important to me."

Her voice sounded sad as she said this. It wasn't easy when friendships were ruined. On the contrary, it really hurt.

She packed up her school things with a melancholy sigh. She just couldn't concentrate anymore today. Quickly, she left Diablo's stall. She glanced at her watch and saw that she still had a half-hour before she had to leave for home. She decided to muck out a few stalls and spread the straw, so that Jake would have less to do. He hadn't been looking very well lately. She would have to speak to her parents about that. Maybe they would have some idea as to what was wrong with him.

Just as she got to Dunja's stall, Lillian arrived. The girl was two years older than Ricki and the proud owner of Doc Holliday.

"Hey, Ricki! What are you still doing here? You're usually on your way home by now."

"Hi, Lillian."

"Isn't Jake here?"

"Yeah, but he isn't looking good lately. Maybe he's coming down with the flu or something."

"Oh, and that's why you're doing his work today?" Lillian went to Holli and greeted him warmly.

"Well, old boy, you're getting fat! I think I'll have to ride you more often, or else I'll have to find someone who will ride you as well. If I only knew who to ask."

48

"Cathy!" Ricki exploded spontaneously.

"What?"

"I said, Cathy! Let Cathy ride Holli, and you will make her the happiest person in the world—with the exception of us, of course."

"Why?" Lillian felt a little pressured. Actually, she hadn't really meant what she said about someone else riding Holli. She was only joking with her horse.

"Why? Because your Holli is Cathy's favorite horse. She'd do anything to ride him."

"Really?" Lillian looked confused at Ricki.

"Lily, you must have noticed!"

"Honestly, cross my heart, I didn't know that Cathy was so fond of old Doc."

"But it's true!" Ricki said, squeezing past the older girl. "Let me through. One more stall, then I've really got to go. Tell Jake that the stalls are finished up to and including Frisbee's."

"Sure, Ricki. You've been riding your devil for quite a while now. Say, want to go out riding with me tomorrow?"

Ricki's eyes lit up. "A ride in the snow? Wonderful! I think Diablo, and I are ready to try it together. Besides, the snow will soften the fall if anything goes wrong."

"What do you mean 'fall'? No one who rides with me falls—is that clear?" Both girls laughed.

"That's all right with me," said Ricki, beaming. "When should we go?"

Lillian thought a moment. "I think if we leave about 3:30 or 4 p.m., we could ride for about an hour and be back before it got too dark."

"Cool!" Ricki was ecstatic. "I've really got to go, otherwise there will be trouble at home, and since Christmas I'm not used to that anymore."

49

Quickly, she emptied the manure cart for the last time today and gave Diablo a final stroke across his nose on her way out.

"We're going riding outside tomorrow—in the snow! So get ready, my boy. Until tomorrow, then."

She grabbed her grooming basket and ran out. "See you tomorrow, Lillian," she yelled on her way past. A glance at the clock showed her that she would really have to pedal fast if she wanted to be home on time.

*

"You say Jake doesn't look well? What's wrong with him?" Marcus, with genuine concerned, asked his daughter across the dinner table. He wasn't at all pleased with Ricki's news.

"I thought you might know something. Jake was acting really strangely yesterday afternoon. He actually fell asleep on the bench in the stable, and he didn't wake up until I was done with the stalls."

"What? You took care of all those horses? Don't tell me you pushed that heavy manure cart and mucked out all the stalls!" Brigitte Sulai's worry for her older child was visible on her face. "You know what Doctor Evans said!"

"Yeah, yeah, I should be careful! But it wasn't that hard, really. I thought, if Jake—"

"Okay, okay! Ricki is still alive and the bone is fine," said Marcus, trying to head off a possible argument between his wife and daughter. "Can we get back to Jake?"

"Right. Today I noticed that his hands were really shaking, and, oh yeah, yesterday he couldn't breathe well," recalled Ricki.

"That doesn't sound good at all. I think I'll drive over to

50

the stable after dinner and look in on him," decided Marcus. Brigitte nodded in agreement.

"If he's really bad, I'll drive him to the doctor's. Doctor Shepherd has night duty this week."

"May I go with you?" asked Ricki nervously. But she knew what her father's answer would be before he said anything.

"Okay, okay, Dad, you don't have to say anything! I know! I was in the stable long enough for today. I should take a shower and finish my homework. I'm supposed to be well rested for school tomorrow morning! Right?"

Marcus laughed. "You can do your own preaching in the future. You seem to know exactly what is right."

Harry, who had been listening to the conversation and was unusually quiet, became very distressed. "Is Grandpa Jake going to die?" he burst out.

Ricki and her parents paled. The little boy had said what the three of them had been thinking during the whole evening. After all, Jake was elderly, and it was getting harder and harder for him to take care of the horses lately. His trouble breathing, the exhaustion, and the intense shaking of his hands seemed to be indications of an illness, and at his age, all illnesses were serious.

"Well, you know," Brigitte began, stroking her son's hair lovingly. She chose her words carefully. "You know, Jake is getting along in years, and everyone has to die sometime—"

"You, too?"

Brigitte swallowed. "Yes, me too, but I think there is still lots of time until then."

Harry stared at the food on his plate, which he had hardly touched. "But I don't want Grandpa Jake to die!" Then he began to sob loudly. Brigitte held him in her arms and stroked his back, but it took a long time for him to calm down.

Ricki pushed her chair away from the table and got up. "Excuse me, but I feel really sick all of a sudden. I think I'll lie down."

Her parents nodded understandingly. They had lost their appetites too.

As Ricki lay in bed later, she heard her father's car drive away. She was relieved that Marcus was going to look in on Jake. If he were really sick, her dad would take him to the doctor immediately.

"Dear God," she prayed that evening, "don't let Jake die. He is such a good man, and Diablo still needs him, and we need him too. We would really miss him. Please, please, let Jake be okay."

With tears in her eyes, Ricki sank into a deep and restless sleep that brought her anything but sweet dreams.

*

At exactly 3 a.m. the next day, Ricki was at the stable. Brigitte had agreed that she could go to the stable right from school, provided she did most of her homework during her lunch break.

At the stable door Ricki ran into Lillian, who waved merrily with a carrot.

"Well, everything okay?"

"Of course!"

They ran happily down the corridor. Ricki couldn't wait. She groomed Diablo quickly, and 20 minutes later both horses stood, saddled and ready, in front of their stalls. The girls tied their warm scarves around their necks, put on a second sweater under their parkas, and clamped their gloves under their arms. Before they could put them on, they had to tighten the girths outside, but then they would be ready.

The brilliant sunny winter weather seemed perfect for a ride on their wonderful horses.

Doc Holliday, with his white coat, was in complete contrast to Ricki's black horse, whose silhouette was sharp against the gleaming snowy landscape. The horses were as excited as their riders. Such a ride in the fresh air was something completely different from the dreary rounds in the dusty riding ring. And there was so much to see.

Diablo was completely absorbed in listening and observing. Curious, he watched everything that moved around him. After first being somewhat cautious, Ricki gave him more freedom. She enjoyed letting him lower his head and plow through the snow with his nose. Of course, every once in a while, he jumped a bit to the side when the snow—which had started to melt—fell suddenly from the branches overhead. But Ricki was secure in the saddle; she could enjoy his harmless pranks.

Doc Holliday wasn't disturbed by anything. He had often ridden this way with Lillian, and he knew every turn, crook and cranny. Lillian turned her head to the sun and let the sunshine warm her face. The sunlight made her sleepy, and she imagined how wonderful it would be to close her eyes and let Doc Holliday lead her. But she knew that could be dangerous. Even the calmest horse could become spooked, and an unprepared rider could have difficulties controlling him and be in danger.

Ricki was lost in thought too. She was still very worried about Jake who, according to her father, had refused to see a doctor. The girl realized that she hadn't seen him at the stable today at all. She became uneasy, but she tried to remain calm. Jake had probably just taken a nap after lunch. She held on to this idea and tried to concentrate on the ride.

"Look over there, in front of us." Lillian stretched out her arm and pointed to a large glittering surface of ice on which there was a gathering of ducks. "The lake is frozen solid."

Ricki followed Lillian's gaze and took in the breathtakingly idyllic picture.

"Wow, that is beautiful," she said with feeling. "I don't think I've ever been here in winter. In the summer I come here often to go swimming. Brrr, I can't believe those creatures aren't freezing."

"Can you ice-skate?"

"No, but I'll bet it's fun. Can you?"

Lillian nodded. "I've been skating since I was 7 years old. I was here two days ago in the afternoon, but there were so many people that I left about half an hour later. You have to come in the evening, when there are only a few adults. I'm surprised the lake is empty today. In this wonderful weather, there are usually lots of people here."

Diablo perked up his ears, and Ricki laughed.

"Oh, Diablo probably goes out on the ice in the afternoons! Now I know why he has been standing in the stall looking so groggy the past few days. He probably overdid it ice-skating!"

Lillian looked thoughtful, as though she had something important she wanted to say. But she changed her mind and instead returned Ricki's smile and extended an invitation. "If you'd like, we could come here together and skate sometime. You can have my old skates. They'd probably fit you."

"Wow, I'd love to. Thanks a lot." Ricki's heart jumped. It was really nice to have the feeling of friendship again.

The girls rode through a long stretch of woods, and they had to duck down often to avoid the snow from the branches overhead. Ricki imagined a magical forest just like this, with a white glistening landscape and powdered trees that stood out like giants against the bright blue sky.

Now a lacy fairy should glide down from a tree and a mythical unicorn should appear from behind a large fir, thought Ricki, dreaming.

Silently enjoying the stillness of the clear winter day, the girls rode through the woods, taking a wide circular route, before they returned to the stable. It was nearly 5 p.m., and dusk was just beginning to replace the sunshine in the sky.

Totally happy, Ricki jumped down from the saddle. She wouldn't have dreamt that Diablo was such a great horse for riding trails. She knew for certain that she would never trade him for any other horse in the world.

As they were leading their horses back to the stalls, Ricki was greatly relieved to see Jake in one of the stalls. The way he was working with the pitchfork, she figured he must be feeling a lot better.

*

Over the next few weeks Ricki and Diablo went riding outside a lot. She was often alone because Lillian didn't always have time to go with her. Usually Ricki chose to ride across the fields, so that she could get home without crossing any streets. She liked to stop at her house to get carrots and apples for Diablo before continuing on to the stable. Diablo got to know the trail by heart and soon could bring his rider home without any guidance.

On these solitary rides, Ricki had a plenty of time to

think. She wondered why Cathy had rejected Lillian's generous offer to let her ride Doc Holliday without comment after two days of thinking it over. Ricki just couldn't understand it. After all, Holli was Cathy's favorite horse. She didn't come to the riding academy very often now, and Lark was hardly there at all anymore.

What's going on with those two? Ricki wondered often, but she couldn't come up with an explanation. She didn't think it had anything to do with her and Diablo. On the other hand, she noticed that Kevin was often at the riding academy and had even begun to show an interest in riding lessons. She was very glad about that, because she had come to really like him.

He had been so happy for her when she had called him on Christmas to tell her about Diablo, and he helped her with her heavy schoolbag when her arm was in the sling. He even opened up more about his horse, Leonardo, who had died so tragically.

When Ricki became distressed about the animosity of her two best friends and some of her classmates, he was the one she talked to about it. He listened to her and tried to cheer her up when she was feeling blue.

"Don't worry about it," he said. "If you really are friends with Cathy and Lark, you'll all survive this and be even better friends than before!"

But the more often she was with Kevin, the cooler the two girls were toward her. When he started to help her with her schoolwork, their jealousy became even more apparent. They envied her happiness with Diablo and with Kevin, and they tried to ruin it by doing petty, spiteful things to hurt her.

For example, one day Ricki found her favorite barrette lying broken on the floor of the dressing room after gym class. Then the photos of Diablo that she had tucked in her notebook to show Kevin at school were discovered torn. And when some money went missing in homeroom, the girls spread a rumor that Ricki had stolen it, pointing to the fact that she appeared at school two days later with a pretty new bracelet as evidence.

"I didn't steal the money," she declared angrily, when their homeroom teacher confronted her in front of her classmates. He had received an anonymous note concerning the money. "The bracelet is a gift from my grandmother."

Lark snorted contemptuously. "Grandmother! That's a laugh!"

Mr. Bradford gave her a scolding glance, but he didn't really believe Ricki either.

He advised her to put the money back unnoticed in order to avoid an embarrassing talk with the school principal. However, he said, he had to inform her parents.

"That's so mean! I just can't believe it!" Ricki couldn't calm down, and Kevin shook his head in disbelief when she told him at lunch what happened.

"Who started this rumor?"

"Who do you think? I can think of two people right away!"

"You don't think that they—"

"Yes, I do! I think it was precisely those two. Man, I could just kill them. And then Mr. Bradford—if he thinks I'm going to return the $ 50 to the class fund, he's crazy. That would be like a confession. Oh no, no—I'm not going to do that!"

Furious, she grabbed her backpack and stomped out of the cafeteria. She wanted to get away from the source of this unfair treatment as quickly as possible.

Kevin watched her leave with sympathy. Then he turned and looked Lark and Cathy straight in their eyes.

Sitting at the next table, Lark grinned at him challengingly, and Cathy blushed under his glance.

"My God, you two should be ashamed of yourselves," he said softly, his voice dripping with contempt. Then he left the lunchroom as well.

"I have no idea what he's talking about!" Lark poked Cathy in the ribs with an artificial laugh.

"Come on, let's get out of here before they start to suspect us." A giggle followed the two of them, as other classmates broke up.

*

"What's going on with you, today?" Lark asked Cathy as they made their way to class.

"Stop it, Lark," complained her friend, staring straight ahead.

"Are you mad?" Lark wouldn't let it go and Cathy was beginning to feel very uncomfortable.

"No, but it just isn't right, what's happening to Ricki."

"Oh, you are being so noble! 'What's happening to Ricki'," she imitated Cathy. Then she abruptly stopped walking and grabbed Cathy's arm. "Look, she deserves to have some problems. Even you said you've had enough of her 'everything's-just-so-wonderful' attitude."

"Yeah, that's true, but it still isn't fair. She hasn't done anything to anybody. Or is it a crime to own a horse and have a boyfriend?"

"Oh, no?" Lark sneered. "That's funny, especially coming from you! You, who practically melt every time you see Kevin. How many times are you going to have to wink at him before he gets the point?!"

Cathy blushed. "Lark, you're mean! Worse than mean!"

"Of course, are you just noticing that? But you can run after Ricki and ask her to forgive you. Maybe she'll even let you scrape out Diablo's hooves!"

Lark's hurtful words stung. Cathy had tears in her eyes.

"And one more thing—maybe you'd like to ride Lillian's Holli after all. Then you'd be reunited with your precious Ricki!"

Cathy decided not to answer. She remembered only too well the conversation she'd had with Lark following Lillian's offer.

"I can ride Holli!" Cathy had told her ecstatically. But Lark was anything but happy about it.

"You can't do that to me! We used to do everything together. And now Ricki has her own horse, and you can ride Holli. Do you both think I'm just going to let you exclude me? You guys don't care about our friendship anymore. If you accept that offer, what kind of a friend would you be?"

Lark actually managed to make Cathy feel guilty. And she keep up the pressure to prevent Cathy from even thinking about going back to Ricki.

"If you think I'm going to let you walk all over me and push me aside just so you can have your fun, you're mistaken. You'll find out the hard way what I'm like. You see how Ricki's life is becoming miserable, so you'd better believe that the same thing will happen to you if you decide I'm not good enough for you to hang with anymore!"

Cathy stared at Lark. She was shocked. Had Lark just threatened her? What happened to the lighthearted, easygoing girl she knew? She had changed so much. Cathy was intimidated and almost afraid of Lark now. Worried that what Lark had made happen to Ricki would happen to her, she decided to reject the offer to ride Holly.

On the same day that Ricki was suspected of theft, Kevin visited her in Diablo's stall for the first time. After that, they were almost always together. They came and went together, gossiped and laughed, groomed Diablo until he shone, hung out in Diablo's stall, where Kevin helped Ricki with math. When it came time to shoe Diablo, Kevin would hold up the horse's hooves so that he could take some of the heavy weight from Ricki's shoulders.

Jake frequently watched the two of them, and came to the conclusion that Ricki and Kevin were very much alike.

When Marcus asked the stable master what he thought of Ricki's boyfriend, Jake was enthusiastic. "Kevin? He's great. Don't worry about him. He's a nice guy—very responsible and down to earth—and he is a good influence on her. You must have noticed that her grades have improved."

Ricki's father nodded. "That's true. She studies, does her homework on time and, she tells me, she finally understands math. Her last test grades were all at least B's and C's, which is great for her!"

Jake nodded his approval. "Yeah, Diablo and Kevin are a good team for Ricki. She's blooming, seems to be very happy, and Kevin is very special to her."

"How do you know that?" Marcus Sulai glanced at his old friend, who smiled and said, "Well, he was allowed to ride Diablo, and up to now, Ricki hasn't let anyone else ride him!"

It was true. After half an hour in the ring, Ricki had dismounted and called Kevin down from the gallery. Not sure what Ricki wanted, he entered the ring with some hesitation, but Ricki just pressed the reins into his hand.

"It's your turn," she said, and walked over to the railing door.

"Hey, what's that supposed to mean?" called Kevin after

her. She knew that he didn't want to ride ever again. Observe riding lessons—yes; but ride himself—never!

"It's your turn, I said. Didn't you hear me?" Ricki glanced back over her shoulder and stopped walking. She thought she knew what Kevin was feeling.

Undecided, he stood there and tried to get his emotions and thoughts under control. The horse in front of him was one of the most wonderful horses he had ever known, and he was waiting for him to mount. On the other hand, he had made a promise to Leonardo that he would never ride another horse. He wanted to honor his memory in that way.

Kevin stood facing Diablo, rubbed the horse's forehead absentmindedly, and looked at him in desperation.

"Even if I wanted to, I can't," he whispered hoarsely.

"Believe me, if Leonardo were here now, he would heave you in the saddle with his hooves." Ricki had come back quietly and now stood behind her friend. He was startled by her words but didn't turn around.

"I can't," he said between tight lips, but Ricki gently put her hand on his shoulder.

"Yes, you can. Not only *can* you, you *have* to. You owe that to Leonardo. Show him that you haven't forgotten anything that you learned through him. Prove to him that nothing and nobody could destroy your love for horses. Prove to him that you are still willing to take a stand against cruel treatment of horses—and riding is a part of all that. You have to ride, Kevin, so that your life becomes whole again. Without riding, you're only half of a person. Do you understand?" She pressed her hand more firmly on his shoulder.

The boy took a deep breath and swallowed. He turned around to face his friend, and Ricki nodded to him encouragingly.

"Believe me, Leonardo would want this. I'm sure that wherever he is, he knows he has a place in your heart that no other horse can take away from him."

Kevin couldn't look at her. He kept his head down, his eyes full of tears, but a soft "thanks," spoken in a voice that was shaking, made Ricki's heart beat faster.

Inside, she celebrated. She'd done it! Kevin would ride again, and she was glad that his first ride in a long, long time would be on Diablo, a wonderful horse, in honor of another wonderful and unforgettable animal—in memory of Leonardo.

Chapter 5

"Something's wrong with Diablo," Ricki complained as she brought the horse back to his stall after a riding session.

Kevin, who had been waiting for her there, frowned. "Why do you say that? He looks like he always does, he eats as much as usual, he isn't lame. What do you mean?"

"I can't tell you exactly what it is," Ricki said, reflecting. "Something is different, but I just can't figure out what it is. Maybe it's just a feeling, but I have the impression—how should I put it—that he's already exhausted by the time I come for our ride. You know, as if he had been running for hours before I showed up."

Kevin took Ricki's concern very seriously, but he laughed in order to relieve her fears. "I'd like to see the person who could saddle and ride Diablo in front of Jake! He'd kill him."

Ricki laughed half-heartedly—she wasn't in the mood for feeble attempts at bravado.

"That's true. But Jake isn't always in the stable, and lately he's been acting strangely—not nearly as talkative and outgoing as he usually is. It's as though he's trying to avoid people. Apparently, he doesn't feel like visiting us anymore; he keeps inventing new excuses every time my mother invites him to dinner. Even Daddy says that it's become almost impossible to talk with him. He's turned into a real grouch, and no one knows why."

Kevin didn't know the answer either, but he wanted to find out what was causing Diablo's tiredness and Jake's strange behavior. There was nothing he wouldn't do to help Ricki with her problems. She was his best friend. She had led him back to the joy of riding, which had been absent from his life for so long, so he would do whatever was necessary. He decided to observe the elderly stable master and Ricki's horse; maybe he would learn something. Ricki didn't need to know about it, however.

*

"By the way, I ran into your homeroom teacher today," Ricki's dad said to her at dinner.

She looked up in surprise. "And what did old Bradford have to say?"

"Well, he told me what you are doing right now in class, and how many students—"

"C'mon, don't make me beg you." Ricki interrupted this boring part of the conversation.

"Okay." Marcus became serious. "He was very happy that you refilled the class fund—"

"What? The money has turned up again?" Ricki was very excited.

"Listen, Ricki, I don't know what—"

"Wait a minute! Before you go on, I'd like to clear something up!" Ricki looked her father straight in the eyes. "I didn't steal that money, and I didn't put it back! I have no idea what he's talking about!"

Ricki then told her father and mother everything that had

64

happened in school over the last few weeks and mentioned her suspicions that Lark and Cathy had something to do with it. Her parents listened closely without interrupting her. They didn't doubt Ricki's innocence, but they weren't comfortable with the idea that the two girls they had known so long, and had welcomed in their house so often, could really have been so vindictive that they would have done something to ruin their daughter's reputation.

"It's true that jealousy and envy can make people do mean things," suggested Brigitte. "But you have to be careful with accusations, if you're not absolutely sure who did what. At any rate, I'm going to talk with Mr. Bradford tomorrow and make it clear that our daughter is not a thief. What is clear, however, is that the person who put the money back wanted to make it seem like Ricki had returned the $ 50 to avoid the consequences. That's really the limit!"

Brigitte was visibly upset. Marcus put his hand on her arm to calm her.

"I think you should talk to Mr. Bradford first, and then we'll see what happens."

Harry, who had listened closely and was fascinated by the whole mystery, chimed in, "I could take my Sherlock Holmes kit to school and dust the money for fingerprints."

Ricki grinned. "Did you ever consider, oh great master detective, that the perpetrator might have worn gloves?"

Disappointment was evident in her brother's face. "I forgot all about that possibility."

"That's all right, Harry. I toyed with that idea myself," Brigitte said, affectionately smoothing back her son's unruly hair.

Marcus turned back to Ricki. "Well, in spite of this unpleasantness, there is something for you to be happy about. Your teacher is very satisfied with your performance at school. Your homework could be a little neater, but he's just pleased that you turn it in on time. And he has discovered that you have a voice."

"A voice? I don't understand."

"Well, that you participate in class and work with the others in class. Apparently, you didn't use to do that—or seldom did," her father explained.

Ricki beamed. "It's all because of Diablo," she said. And Harry added, "Because of Diablo and her true love!"

Ricki gave him one of her superior big-sister glances.

"Diablo is my true love!"

"Hah, I don't mean him. I was speaking of Kevin."

A crumpled-up napkin was thrown at his head.

"Ha ha, Ricki's in love, Ricki's in love!"

Harry almost fell under the table from laughing. Marcus tried to hide his grin. Ricki was bright red and stared at her plate, while Brigitte tried desperately to get her son to shut up. She knew how embarrassing it was for Ricki that her younger brother had exposed her feelings for Kevin to the entire family. Ricki would have liked to go to her room or at least crawl under the table, but she wasn't going to give her brother that satisfaction.

"Harry, that's enough!" Brigitte's voice was stern now. But her son couldn't stop laughing. He laughed until there were tears in his eyes and his stomach hurt.

Just then, the doorbell rang, and Marcus went to answer it, returning a few moments later with Kevin in tow. The sight of Ricki's friend sent Harry off on another laughing fit.

"Good evening," Kevin said politely as he nodded to Ricki's parents. "What's the matter with him?" he asked, pointing at Harry.

Ricki blushed with embarrassment. "My brother just decided that you are my true love—next to Diablo, of course."

Kevin beamed at her, then he turned to Harry and said, "Well, it's about time someone noticed!"

Immediately everyone was silent.

"What?" Ricki's brother asked nonplussed.

"Of course," replied Kevin coolly.

Marcus asked, "Should we congratulate you?"

"Marcus!" Brigitte chastised, shaking her head to warn that he was embarrassing Kevin. But Kevin remained relaxed.

"We'll let you know when we decide to marry," he quipped, playing along with Marcus's teasing.

Ricki wished she could just disappear, but she saw no escape. She got up finally and mumbled something about a math problem that Kevin had to explain to her, and then she pulled her friend out of the kitchen and up the stairs.

"I guess I'm going to have to get used to the idea that our Ricki isn't a little kid anymore," grinned Marcus.

Brigitte countered immediately, "And I have to get used to the idea that my husband sometimes acts like a little kid!"

*

"I'm sorry," Ricki apologized to Kevin when they in her room, out of hearing range of nosey family members. "Brothers and fathers can be horrible sometimes."

"Why? Because they practically had us setting a wedding date? Well, admittedly, it may be a little early, but otherwise—"

"KEVIN! Don't you start! Why did you come here anyway? We just said good-bye about an hour ago. By the way, the money that was missing from the class fund has turned up. Mr. Bradford told my father."

67

Kevin plunked himself down on the large floor pillow near Ricki's desk. "Good, then everything is cleared up."

"Nothing is cleared up, but let's forget about that, it just makes me mad. Tell me why you're here." She looked at him expectantly.

"I was thinking about what you said at the stable. You know, about your feeling that something was wrong. Well, I thought of something. I wouldn't have made anything out of it if you hadn't put me on the trail with your concerns."

Ricki felt her legs get weak, and she sat down on her bed, without taking her eyes off Kevin.

"C'mon, tell me!"

"Okay! As you know, I was in the stable early Sunday morning. We had agreed that I should ride Diablo for an hour in the morning, since you didn't have time until the afternoon."

"That's right. What else?" Ricki was growing anxious.

"I came into the stable, said hello to Diablo, like always and, when I started to go into his stall to begin grooming him, I noticed that the door wasn't shut. At first, I thought maybe Jake had forgotten to close it, but when I asked him he got really mad. He said he wasn't that senile, and so on. There must have been someone else in the stall with Diablo."

Ricki paled. "But no one's supposed to be in there!" For a moment, she was silent, but then her worst fears came out. "Not Cooper—?"

Kevin shook his head. "No, I don't think so. He wouldn't dare go into the stall anymore…and besides, if he had been with Diablo, he would have used his whip, just as he always did. But your horse was completely calm and relaxed when I approached him. It couldn't have been Cooper."

"But who was it then? I'm going to ask Jake tomorrow who was in the stable. And then I'll talk to everyone and ask them if they were with Diablo."

"Good idea," agreed Kevin. "It will probably turn out to be something totally harmless," he said.

"I hope you're right," Ricki said, more to herself than to her friend. "But I have a bad feeling about this."

Kevin looked at her intently. "We have to observe everything and everyone at the stable very carefully from now on. Maybe then we'll figure out what's going on."

"Yeah, we have to," Ricki agreed. "I'm going to include Jake in our plan. After all, he's with the horses almost all day. If it concerns Diablo, we can be sure he'll keep his eyes and ears open."

For a few minutes they sat quietly, each with their own thoughts. Then Kevin uncrossed his legs, got up stiffly, and stretched.

"I've got to leave now," he said, and Ricki got up as well to accompany him downstairs to the front door.

"Did I tell you that my parents are getting a divorce?" he said, almost too calmly, when they were in the hall.

"What?" Ricki said, stunned. "Why?"

"Mom just can't stand living with my father anymore. He yells all the time, and he's impossible to please. To be honest, I'm glad they're separating."

"Well, it would be awful for me if my parents ... but I guess with you it's different. After all, what happened to Leonardo was your father's fault."

Kevin ground his teeth as he always did when he was reminded of the death of his horse. Silently he nodded, then he added, "Now Mom and I have to find another place to live—as cheap as possible, since the farm and the horses belong to my father, and he will pay us as little as possible."

Slowly the two of them walked down the stairs. Kevin called his good-byes to the Sulais, who were watching TV in the living room, and bundled himself into his jacket and tied his scarf.

Outside the steps, Kevin suddenly turned around toward Ricki: "Am I really your true love?"

"No way!" answered Ricki a little too quickly. She was glad that it was dark so Kevin couldn't see that she was blushing.

"Too bad," he said, and in that moment his voice sounded like a grownup's. "I like you a lot," he added before he got on his bike and headed home.

*

It was the middle of March, and Diablo's condition had hardly changed at all. Some days, he was as fit as he had been in the early days when Ricki rode him, but there were days when he didn't have any of the usual pep in his gait that had made him such an elegant horse to ride. This didn't happen often, but nevertheless, Ricki was sufficiently concerned and asked Dr. Hofer for his opinion.

"Organically, he's in perfect shape," was the vet's diagnosis.

Although Ricki, Kevin, and Jake focused their attention on Diablo and his surroundings, they never discovered anything that would account for Diablo's exhaustion. The situation continued to puzzle them—until the day they found a small clue.

Ricki had left the stable on a Saturday evening, after she'd ridden Diablo, as she did every day. She had hung her saddle, in the proper manner, over her stand in the tack

70

room. When she arrived with Kevin the next morning, her saddle stand was empty, but her saddle and bit hung neatly on another stand nearby.

"Huh, what's going on?" she asked perplexed. "I'm sure that I hung my things on my stand yesterday."

Kevin looked at the saddle and bit for a long time and then he said thoughtfully, "I noticed this once before, but I didn't think anything of it. I just thought you had mixed up the stands. They all look alike."

"I didn't mix anything up," growled Ricki. "There's something fishy going on, let me tell you…very fishy! Someone is using my saddle gear on a regular basis. Just wait until I find the person responsible!"

Ricki examined the girth and the straps for the bit. "Strange…nothing is different. I don't get it."

Shaking her head, she got her things and carried them to Diablo's stall. His greeting was a little weak. "Well, my little devil, what's wrong with you today? You look like you've been walking all night. Why is your coat so matted on your neck? You're not sick, are you?"

Ricki turned to Kevin. "I think I'm going to call Dr. Hofer again," she said, upset.

Kevin tried to lift her spirits. "Oh, nonsense, he doesn't look sick at all. Maybe he saddled himself last night and then—" As he was talking, he realized what he had just said. Ricki, her eyes wide with sudden understanding, also realized the importance of Kevin's remark.

"Of course," she said excitedly. "That's it! … that's it exactly! My God, someone is saddling my horse after hours and riding around—that's just unbelievable! No wonder he's tired all the time!"

Ricki couldn't bear to think about what could have happened to her horse on these late-night rides. She thought it was so irresponsible of this ghost rider to take any horse out of his stall and ride him.

"We have to do something," said Kevin, following Ricki back to the tack room with her saddle. She didn't feel like riding anymore today. Especially since she wanted to spare her horse, who now stood dozing in his stall. After all, she didn't know how long he had been ridden last night.

"Now I understand about the open stall door. The ghost rider forgot to close it!" Ricki nodded in agreement at Kevin's words.

"We should ask the other horse owners if they've noticed anything. Maybe their horses are being ridden as well. If so, we should get all the riders together and then take turns guarding the stalls at night."

The two were silent for a few minutes as they thought about a plan. After Ricki hung her saddle on the appropriate stand, they started slowly walking back to Diablo's stall.

"No," Kevin said finally, shaking his head. "The more people who know about it, the less chance we have of finding out who did it. And, if we're unlucky, we could tip off the ghost rider. Then he would be warned, and we wouldn't be able to catch him."

"That's true. He probably wouldn't come back to the stalls at night, but at least Diablo would be left in peace."

"Yeah, but you wouldn't be!" Kevin countered. "You'd have to continue living with the fear that what happened with Cooper might begin again someday—wouldn't you?"

Ricki looked at her horse. "I suppose so. I probably wouldn't be able to sleep nights."

"We have to think of something else—but what?"

They squatted in front of Diablo's stall. It was noticeably quiet in the stable today. Somewhere in the distance they could hear the stable master with his feeding bowls.

72

Suddenly Ricki and Kevin looked at each other. "Jake!" they shouted simultaneously.

"We have to tell Jake our plans. He lives above the stable. If anyone has the opportunity to find out something about the ghost rider without being noticed, he does. I'm sure he'll keep it to himself."

"I think so, too," agreed Kevin as he got up. "Okay, let's talk to him right now. After all, it concerns Diablo's well-being."

Ricki stood up, brushing bits of oats and hay from her jeans. She didn't like the idea that Jake would have to be awake at night, especially since he hadn't been looking well, but she couldn't think of any other solution at the moment. The two started off to figure out a strategy with Jake.

They found him in the feed room, where he was mixing powdered vitamins, health food, and oats for each individual horse. He reacted a little brusquely to Ricki's greeting and didn't even acknowledge Kevin; he just continued mixing the feed. But when she told him about her suspicions, he flinched and turned around slowly. He was even paler than she'd seen him lately. Ricki was horrified.

"Jake, aren't you feeling well? My God, sit down."

The old stable master shook off her hand as she tried to help him to a stool in the corner.

"Let me alone! I'm fine!" Breathing heavily, he leaned on the feed bin and closed his eyes. "So what do you want to do?" he asked softly.

Ricki exchanged looks with Kevin, like maybe they shouldn't have bothered Jake with any of this. Kevin responded with a resigned shrug.

"What now?" Jake was becoming irritated.

"Actually, we thought that maybe you … since you live

above the stable … but forget it, we'll think of something else."

Ricki grabbed Kevin's sleeve and quickly pulled him into the corridor before Jake could answer.

"Did you see how he looks? We can't ask him to do a nightshift. If I only knew what was wrong with him. He's been gruff and impossible for weeks. When you look at him, you feel as though he's about to collapse."

Kevin nodded in agreement. "I wonder how he manages to do all the work in the stalls every day. Twenty horses are a lot to care for!"

"Come," said Ricki. "Let's go outside. I need some fresh air."

"Me, too," Kevin agreed. "Maybe we can come back later this afternoon. Then we could help with the feeding and clearing out the stalls. I don't think Jake will mind."

Ricki was already on her bike. "That's a good idea. Say, do you feel like having an early dinner at our house? Mom makes a big meal on Sunday afternoon and, anyway, she always makes way too much food."

Kevin was delighted. "Yeah, I'd really like to. I'll just give my mother a call when we get to your place so she knows where I am."

"Great, then we'll have a lot more time to think," the girl said, and she rode off in front of Kevin so he couldn't see her eyes shining.

*

After the two had left the feed room, Jake sat down heavily on the wooden stool. Ricki's suspicions made his chest tighten and he had a hard time breathing—a symptom he'd been experiencing for the past few weeks. The old man realized that his body was sending him signals that he was

74

sick. He knew he should see a doctor, but he was afraid. He was afraid the doctor would tell him he was dying. This fear paralyzed him and made him incapable of telling anyone. It also made him avoid people. He knew that the people who loved him would take him to a hospital immediately if they knew how sick he was. So Jake distanced himself from Ricki and her family. That way they would leave him alone and wouldn't notice how ill he had become.

*

Ricki's parents were surprised when Ricki came in through the door with Kevin.

"Hello, Kevin, how nice to see you again," Marcus Sulai smiled, and welcomed him in. "Let me take your coat. You're becoming a permanent fixture around here, aren't you?" he said, reaching for a hanger.

The boy blushed and was about to answer, but Ricki answered for him.

"Hey—I invited Kevin to dinner. Is that okay with you guys? After all, there's usually a lot left over!"

Brigitte Sulai laughed. "If the plan is to rid me of my leftovers, I don't mind at all."

"Cool. Thanks, Mom. Can Kevin make a fast telephone call?"

"Of course. He can talk as slowly as he wants, for all I care. Come back in 20 minutes. I think the roast will be done by then."

"Okay, we'll see you in a bit." Ricki ushered Kevin out of the front hall and in the direction of the telephone.

Brigitte and Marcus smiled at each other knowingly.

"Really a nice boy," Ricki's father said, taking his wife by the arm and together walking back to the kitchen.

"Have you ever doubted your daughter's taste?" teased Brigitte.

"Of course not," replied Marcus, pretending outrage. "A young woman who loves fabulous horses, loves fabulous men as well!"

"Oh no, then I must have done something wrong. I don't have a thing to do with horses, after all—"

"Damn, fell into my own trap." Marcus laughed, defeated. He went to put another place setting on the table, while Brigitte sliced some radishes for the salad.

*

"I think we can't do anything alone," said Kevin, who was leaning casually against the windowsill in Ricki's room. "We can't depend on Jake—it looks like he has his own problems right now—and we can't recruit other riders either. If we do, we won't be able to trap the unknown rider. We need a different plan."

Ricki put her horse-grooming basket neatly in the corner. The rest of her room was fairly tidy as well. After Kevin had visited her for the first time, she had begun to keep her room in order. If he was to visit again, she wanted him to like being in her room.

Right now she was sitting in front of the dresser, on the huge floor pillow. "Yeah, but how?" she wondered out loud and looked at her friend questioningly.

Kevin shrugged. "Maybe we should talk it over with your parents."

"Are you out of your mind? They'll think we're crazy. And if we tell them that we want to watch the stable all night, you can bet they'll lock me in my room as soon as it gets dark!"

"Well, I can't think of anything else, and I don't think it would be a bad thing if one or two adults knew about this."

"Hmm … maybe you're right," said Ricki finally. "I'll put the whole story on the table later."

Kevin grinned. "If you think there will be room among all the salad, roast, potatoes, and vegetables your mother is cooking."

Ricki picked up a magazine and threw it at him. "Oh, you … let's go. The 20 minutes are up anyway."

*

Brigitte and Marcus didn't think their daughter was entirely crazy. They listened attentively and seriously to Ricki's suspicions. The whole story sounded believable, although Marcus thought it was a little unrealistic to think that some stranger could get Diablo out of his stall at night and ride him.

"Maybe there is a simple explanation for the open door in the stall and the mixed-up saddle stands," he said, looking cautiously at Ricki, who glanced across the table at her boyfriend. See, *I told you!* she seemed to be saying.

Kevin shook his head imperceptibly before he turned to Ricki's parents.

"But, Mr. Sulai, why is Diablo tired so often when we ride him?"

"Sore muscles?"

"Nonsense, Daddy! Sore muscles! If a horse has been ridden one to two hours a day for weeks, he's not worn out, nor does he have sore muscles with that kind of regularity! It … it has to be something else. And today there were dry, matted places on Diablo's neck, and I'm sure that his coat was smooth and brushed and groomed yesterday!" *Why doesn't he understand? Or doesn't he want to understand?* wondered Ricki, a little angry.

"Listen, I suggest you continue to observe Diablo carefully and write down everything that seems strange. At some point, your ghost rider will leave a useable clue behind, and then—"

"And then it could be too late for Diablo! Just imagine, what if he stumbles at night, or if—?"

"Ricki…Ricki!" Brigitte put her hand on her daughter's arm to calm her. "Don't imagine the worst."

"Actually, we wanted Jake—"

"How is he? He hasn't been here for ages."

"Well, not so good. He's been acting so strange."

Ricki wanted to get back to the real topic as quickly as possible, but her father was faster.

"I think we have to worry more about Jake than Diablo. I'm not sure it was such a good idea to include him in your plans. That just adds to his concern for Diablo when he worries about his health problems."

Kevin and Ricki exchanged guilty looks. "We didn't think of that until after we told him about Diablo," Ricki admitted sheepishly.

They were relieved when Marcus promised that he would drive them to the stable after they finished eating in order to look around, but also, mainly, to see about Jake.

"After all, you never know," he added, worried.

*

Of course, Ricki's father couldn't turn up anything out of the ordinary when they visited the riding stable. Consequently, he decided the situation wasn't that serious.

78

He didn't get to see Jake that afternoon either. His friend wasn't in the stable, and his apartment door was locked. Marcus drove back home feeling he hadn't accomplished anything except adding to his own worries about Jake.

Days went by, and Ricki and Kevin met every afternoon at the stable to do their homework, usually in Diablo's stall. They went to visit the horse as early as possible and returned home later and later, always hoping to find a clue about the ghost rider. Even though Diablo seemed better, Ricki continued to be terribly worried about her horse, imagining all the awful things that could happen to him at the hands of a stranger.

"I can't stand it anymore!" she said to Kevin in desperation one day, when she noticed that Diablo's bit strap had been tampered with. "If I catch that jerk, I don't know what I'll do to him. It's so irresponsible—not to mention dishonest and unethical!"

"I can't believe that it's one of our club riders, but who else could get into the stalls?" Kevin didn't know what to do either. "Maybe if we ask the board—"

"No way!" Ricki interrupted him. "I don't trust those VIPs anymore, not since Cooper—"

Kevin lowered his eyes, remembering with shame his father's part in the mistreatment of Diablo.

Noticing his discomfort, Ricki quickly added, "Kevin, you aren't responsible for your father's tolerating the cruelty to Diablo. I think the others knew about it too. That's why I don't trust them anymore."

"Tolerated? He actually supported it!" Kevin fumed. Then he turned abruptly and walked briskly down the corridor.

Ricki bit her lip. *I'm an idiot,* she thought. *Why did I have to open that wound again?*

"Kevin," she called after him. "Kevin! Wait!"

When he didn't react, she ran after him and grabbed his hand. He stopped and stood with his back to her. Taking him by the elbows, she forced him to turn around and look at her.

"I'm sorry, Kevin. Please, stay here."

"Why? Why would you want to have anything to do with the son of an animal abuser?" Kevin was bitter. He tried to shake off Ricki's hand, but she held tightly.

"I, because—" Suddenly she got up on her toes and gave him a quick kiss on his cheek. "Because you're my boyfriend, that's why."

Then she left Kevin standing there with a look of surprise on his face, and ran back to Diablo. She pressed her face into his mane, and he nuzzled against her. He loved these cuddles with his owner.

God, I really kissed him. The memory of that spontaneous act hit her like a truck. She felt a little embarrassed. She hoped she hadn't chased Kevin away with her impulsive show of affection.

"Hi, you guys, it's been a long time!" Lillian's happy voice was heard along the corridor. She patted Kevin's shoulder affectionately as she went past him and winked at Ricki, who was looking out of Diablo's stall.

"Hey, Lillian. Are you going riding outside?"

"Sure! How about it? Want to come?"

Somewhat undecided, Ricki looked at Kevin. Actually, they'd planned to ride Diablo in the ring, but now riding outside with Lillian seemed tempting.

"Yeah, I'd like to, but—"

"Go ahead!" Kevin waved her on. "You don't have to stay here because of me."

Ricki was in a dilemma. It was really too bad that Kevin

80

no longer had his own horse to go riding with them. And he had sworn never to saddle one of his father's horses again.

Lillian looked back and forth at the two. After a few seconds, she tapped her forehead with her finger.

"My God, I'm an idiot!" she said quietly, and rolled her eyes. She blinked at Kevin and laughed.

"If there is anything I can do for two people in love, you only need to tell me."

Ricki cleared her throat in embarrassment, while Kevin smiled. "Well, if that's the way it is, good fairy godmother, then please make a horse appear so that I can go riding with you. After all, it's not a good idea for two girls to go riding alone without a man to protect them."

Ricki breathed a sigh of relief. Kevin didn't appear upset by her kiss; in fact, he seemed as happy as usual.

"Oh, if it were only that easy to make horses appear," Lillian groaned.

"That's what I was afraid of. First all this talk about wanting to help, and then you take it all back," Kevin teased.

"What do you mean, take it back?" she asked. She had led Doc Holliday out of his stall and was standing right in front of Kevin. Hesitating just for a moment, she then pressed the reins of her horse into his hand.

"You want a horse so you can go riding with Ricki? Here you go! Holli and I are having our generous day today, and anyway, we always stand by our offers!"

Kevin looked at Lillian, perplexed. "Do you always decide for your horse?" he asked.

"Not always, but when I say stuff without thinking, I always stand by what I said. I think a different rider would be good for Holli. I think I've spoiled him pretty much, and overlooked a lot. Maybe you can get him to stop making some of those little mistakes—"

"And what would they be?" asked Kevin as he rubbed Holli between the ears.

"Well, for example, … for example—oh, I can't think of anything at the moment."

Kevin understood. "Are you sure I should ride Holli?"

Lillian gave him a penetrating look. "Should? You shouldn't do anything! You may, if you want to!"

In the meantime, Ricki had come closer. Thankful, she glanced at Lillian "Lily, you are … you are …"

" … crazy that I don't ride my own horse. C'mon, get going—and stop calling me Lily!"

"Okay, Lily!" Kevin beamed, and the girl playfully punched him in the arm.

"Just so you know … if you ride him, you'll start something!"

"What do you mean?" asked Kevin. But Lillian was looking only at her horse, who was nibbling contentedly on Kevin's shoulder.

"If Holli thinks you're good enough to eat, you'll have to ride him often. Understand? At least two or three times a week. But only when I'm not able to ride him. Okay? So, get going, you two! Have fun … and bring Holli back safely. If anything happens to him, I'll lynch you!"

Lillian gave her horse a big kiss on the nose and then headed off to the riders' lounge. Maybe she would run into another lonesome rider there with whom she could pass the time until Holli was back.

Chapter 6

Astride Doc Holliday, Kevin reveled in his good fortune. And Ricki, seeing Kevin's pleasure with being on horseback, envied, admired, and was grateful for Lillian's spontaneous generosity. Once again she thought about Cathy and Lark. Maybe she could have saved their friendship if she'd shown the same generosity and allowed them to ride Diablo every once in a while. After all, she didn't have a problem with letting Kevin ride him. But then, Kevin was different!

As the two of them rode away from the stable, the animals' coats shone in the brilliant sunshine. This was the first time Ricki and Kevin had gone riding outside together, but they both knew that if what Lillian had suggested came to pass, it wouldn't be the last.

The horses trotted briskly along without any urging. They had been riding for a while when they started down the gravel path along the old railroad tracks. Beneath their hooves the gravel crunched, and the noble animals lowered their necks to breathe in the smell of the beginning of spring.

Snorting, Diablo shook his head and quickened his pace. He would have liked to gallop over the long bordering meadow, but Ricki reined him in.

"Hey, boy. Slow down. Springtime meadows are not racetracks!"

Kevin sensed an unrest in Doc Holliday as well, as they rode beside the meadow.

"Is this Lillian's usual stretch to gallop? Holli is very tense, as though he wants to begin to race at any moment."

Ricki looked at the white horse and just shook her head and shrugged. "No, Lillian doesn't ever ride across meadows. Her parents have a little farm, and she told me her parents always said you have to let meadows alone in the spring and summer so as not to spoil the harvest. And Holli has never acted like this before when she and I rode here together!"

"Well, maybe it's my fault," said Kevin. He let Doc Holliday jump so he could get him back to a normal trotting pace.

"I think it would be better to change our direction." Ricki had a hard time keeping Diablo under control. She couldn't understand why her horse had suddenly become so excitable. The fatigue he had regularly exhibited in the stall was gone.

Kevin pointed ahead. "Look, to the left of that large chestnut tree, there's a fork in the trail. Let's turn there. I know the way. I used to ride there with Leonardo."

"I thought that path led directly to the gravel works." Ricki's arms were beginning to tire. Diablo was straining on the reins.

"It goes past the gravel works and around a big quarry lake to the road. Then it passes the Meyers's farm and then back in the direction of the riding academy."

"Holy cow … and I thought I knew my way around here pretty well. I guess not!" Ricki patted the sweaty neck of her black horse to calm him down, and as she glanced on the ground she noticed something. "Hey, look, there are hoof marks."

"And they lead directly into the meadow. Some horses must have raced through there. Look at the surface of the grass. There are holes in it. Who'd be dumb enough to race on a wet meadow?"

"Diablooo—stop! Are you crazy?" Ricki could hardly keep her seat as the horse tore the reins out of her hands, bit down, and bolted. He raced across the wide meadow at breakneck speed. Ricki was powerless. She could neither hold the horse nor guide him, so she prayed while desperately trying every way she knew to stop her horse.

Kevin turned pale, but before he knew it, Doc Holliday bolted too. *The farmer will kill us, if someone sees us,* he thought as he raced unwillingly behind Ricki.

"Ahhh …" Diablo stopped short and slid on his hind legs.There was a restless tranquility to the air, as if misfortune would present itself at any minute. Suddenly, Kevin screamed.

Ricki pitched forward. The only thing that prevented her from falling was Diablo's neck. Frightened, she turned around and saw Holli with dirty flanks limping slowly toward her. The saddle was empty. "My God, Kevin," she whispered softly. Then she screamed. "Kevin! What happened?"

Diablo allowed her to guide him, and she turned around quickly and trotted back. She jumped down from the saddle six feet in front of Kevin, who was still lying on the ground. She knelt down by her friend as Diablo trotted over to Doc Holliday, who had come to a stop with his front leg held at an angle. They stared at their riders, who made no attempt to catch them.

Kevin kept his eyes closed. The pain in his left ankle seemed to numb him. Everything had happened so fast. He had been concentrating on Ricki and her breathless ride.

85

He had been so worried about what could happen to her that he had paid more attention to Diablo than to the ground.

Holli stepped into a hole, stumbled, and fell while galloping. Kevin had fallen under him and was lucky to have pulled his feet out of the stirrups in time. Slowly he opened his eyes and saw the horrified look on Ricki's face. Her complexion had been completely drained of colour and she seemed as if she was in shock. Finally Kevin opened his mouth to speak. "How's—how's Holli?" he asked quietly with a stammer.

Ricki swallowed hard. "He's limping, but … but what about you?"

When Kevin tried to move his left foot, he groaned with pain. "Crap—" Then he tried to smile but it didn't work; in fact, it looked more like a grimace.

"I think I'm still a little out of practice with riding. I didn't see that darn hole at all. I just hope nothing bad has happened to Holli. Lillian will cut me into eight pieces!"

Shaking, Ricki stretched her hand toward him. "Can you stand up?" she asked, scared but hopeful. But Kevin just shook his head.

"No way," he squeezed out through his tightly pressed lips.

Ricki's heart filled with sympathy as she put her arms around the boy's shoulders. She would gladly have changed places with him. It was unbearable for her to see him in such pain.

Exhausted, Kevin leaned on Ricki. He was glad she was near him. Slowly he turned his gaze toward the horses, who were standing together looking at their riders attentively.

Kevin breathed a sigh of relief when he saw Doc Holliday standing on his injured leg. Luckily, the horse didn't seem to be badly hurt. But he couldn't be sure until Dr. Hofer had examined him. Maybe the leg was sprained or possibly strained, but at least it wasn't broken, and that was the most important thing.

"What should we do now?" Ricki looked around, not knowing the answer. There wasn't a house or a farm anywhere in sight where they could ask for help. "If you could only get up," she said. "Then maybe I could help you get into Diablo's saddle."

But Kevin shook his head. Meanwhile, the pain in his leg seemed to spread throughout his body, and he knew for sure that getting up was out of the question. "Maybe it would be better to let me lie here. You ride back with Holli and Diablo. I'm sure that someone at the stable will have a car and come get me."

"But I can't just let you …"

"We don't have any other choice. Go on, ride! And please hurry," he added as Ricki hesitantly stood up.

She ran over to the horses. Just to be sure, she felt Holli's front leg. It was swollen, but the animal could walk. Slowly she led him to Kevin, who sat up a little so that he could watch her.

"I'm leaving Holli here," Ricki decided. "It hurts him to walk, and I'm sure that he won't go far away from you. If he comes with me it will take forever. With just Diablo, I can be at the stable in about 20 minutes."

Kevin nodded and reached out his hand. "Give me the reins. I'll feel better, if I know Holli can't take off."

Ricki did as Kevin asked, took a deep breath, and mounted her horse.

Diablo didn't know what to think of all this and danced restlessly. With one last glance at Kevin and Holli, Ricki pressed her thighs together and raced off on Diablo.

"Be careful," Kevin murmured after her, before he was overwhelmed by a new wave of pain.

*

The wind made Ricki's eyes tear. Her concern for Kevin caused her to urge Diablo to go as fast as he could, and she was startled by the speed of his pace. On her way back to the stable she took the shortest route through the meadow. Time was of the essence. She took a deep breath of relief when, just 15 minutes later, she recognized the outlines of the riding academy.

"Diablo, my sweetie, thank you! You are the fastest and best horse in the world, but you can't bolt anymore!" She patted his wet neck and jumped out of the saddle.

Before she had even thrown the reins over his neck, the outer door of the riding ring flew open, and Lillian came running out, white-faced.

"I saw you coming. Where's Holli? Has something happened? My God, say something. Where is my horse?" she asked excitedly. Lillian grabbed Ricki's arms and shook her.

"Lillian—Lillian, please, calm down. It's not serious."

"Then tell me what happened!"

Ricki held the girl tightly and tried to look her straight in the eyes. "If you'd let me talk, then I could tell you every-thing."

Lillian closed her eyes and took a deep breath. She held up her hands to show that she was sorry.

"Okay … I'm calm now. What happened?"

Ricki nodded at her. "Let's go into the stalls so that Diablo doesn't catch cold."

As Ricki led her Diablo into his stall, she outlined more

or less what had happened. The few riders that were present listened closely as well.

"We need a car and a horse trailer fast, so that we can go get Kevin and Holli," said Ricki hastily. She began to unsaddle Diablo more quickly than she ever had ever done before.

Twenty-year-old Nick said he was willing to pick up Kevin and Holli, but Lillian just shook her head.

"That won't work. Holli won't get into a trailer ever since my dad had that accident at the tournament when someone hit him from the rear. I'll go with you and lead him home." And she left with the young man immediately.

"Wait!" yelled Ricki after them. "I'm coming, too! You don't know where they are!" Panic-stricken, she glanced at Diablo, who was still sweating after his ride. She would need at least 15 minutes to rub him down, and that meant 15 more minutes of pain and uncertainty for Kevin. But she couldn't let her horse just stand there soaking wet.

"Go! I'll take care of Diablo!" Jake's gravelly voice tore Ricki from her thoughts.

"You're an angel, Jake. Thank you!" she said, embracing the old stable master quickly before running past him to join up with Nick and Lillian.

While Jake slowly and carefully rubbed Diablo's coat with fresh straw and an old towel, Nick drove to the scene of the accident with Ricki and Lillian. From a distance, they could recognize Holli's silhouette standing high against the sky, and in front of him, a little figure that was desperately trying to get up.

When Kevin saw the car, he let himself fall backward and sighed with relief. Finally! The past half hour had seemed like an eternity.

Nick drove over the meadow, leaving deep tracks in the

89

wet ground. Even before the car had fully stopped, Lillian had opened the passenger car door and jumped out. After a short sideward glance at Kevin, she took Holli's reins out of his hands and concentrated on comforting her horse, who greeted her with a gentle snort. Lillian swallowed hard after getting Holli to take a few limping steps, before he stopped again to spare his leg.

"Lily, I'm so sorry," Kevin began, but the girl wouldn't look at him.

"I hate you," she growled softly and buried her head in Holli's mane. It would be a long walk home.

Nick had pulled Kevin up with his strong arms and supported him, so that he could hop the six feet to the car.

Ricki tried to smile and cheer him up. She would have liked to stay by him, but she knew that he would soon be taken care of, and she also knew that she couldn't leave Lillian alone. After all, Holli had bolted after Diablo and had injured himself because of it.

"I'll call you," she said quietly to Kevin, who looked at her thankfully before Nick closed the car door.

"I'm going to drive him to the hospital… . Will you be okay with Holli?"

Ricki shrugged her shoulders. "I sure hope so."

*

Lillian had to go very slowly with Doc Holliday. Every few steps, the horse stopped to rest his leg.

While Nick drove over the meadow back to the road, Ricki ran after Lillian and Holli. She blamed herself for the accident, but she also knew that a wrong step could happen at any time to anyone on an uneven meadow. And when a horse bolted, the rider, no matter how skilled, was helpless.

"Lillian," she began cautiously, but the girl pretended not to hear. "Please, listen to me—"

"What do you want?" Lillian snapped. "You injured my horse, and now I'm supposed to thank you for that?"

"No, but—"

"Leave me alone! Why didn't you go with your boyfriend? I don't need your help, and Holli doesn't either! Come, sweetheart, we have to go on, otherwise we'll be here all night." Gently she coaxed her horse forward a few steps, while Ricki followed with her head down, feeling guilty and remorseful.

She could easily understand Lillian's attitude. She wouldn't have reacted any differently if it had been Diablo instead of Holli. And yet she wanted so much to talk about it with Lillian. But Lillian wouldn't listen to her. Ricki and Kevin had ceased to exist for her. Let them ride other people's horses!

Ricki walked more slowly, letting the distance between them get a little larger. She felt miserable and completely useless. Finally, she bent down to pick up a stone. She wanted to throw her cares away with it. But her gaze fixed on something colorful on the ground about 15 feet from where the green grass of the meadow started.

Slowly she walked toward it. What was it? A moment later, she held a red-and-white-striped ribbon headband in her hands.

How did this get here? she wondered. She realized that she'd seen this ribbon somewhere before, but she couldn't remember where.

*

Lillian was desperate. She'd managed to get Holli to the edge of the meadow, but now he wouldn't take one more

91

step. Sobbing, Lillian leaned against her horse. She had no idea how she could get Holli back home.

Hesitantly Ricki came nearer. "Maybe we should get a trailer—"

"Leave me alone!" Lillian said again.

Ricki started to back off again, but then she knew that one of them had to think logically if they were going to get Doc Holliday back without causing any further injury to his leg.

"I understand that you are really angry at us, but that won't help Holli now. If we don't want to spend the night here, we've got to think of something!"

Ricki paused and then continued. "I'm going to run back to the riding academy and get a trailer. Don't say anything. I know, you said Holli won't go into a trailer, but maybe he would if Diablo is already in it. They like each other."

"I doubt it," said Lillian, but Ricki felt that Holli's owner was ready to try anything. Ricki didn't wait to see if Lillian would say anything. She just started to run, happily escaping Lillian's glares.

"I'll be back as soon as possible," she called over her shoulder.

Oh, brother, she thought while she forcing herself to keep the pace. *On Diablo, the way back seemed short, but if I have to run it, it seems endless.*

She glanced back and saw that Lillian and Doc Holliday were still standing where she'd left them. Ricki pressed her teeth together. Her breath started to rattle loudly from the unusual exertion, and her feet hurt up to her calves from the pressure of her riding boots.

When at last she saw the riding academy she dropped to her knees for a minute to rest. She was at the end of her strength, but her desire to help Lillian and Doc Holliday gave her the drive to make it the rest of the way.

Breathing heavily and with shaking legs, she entered the building. Startled, a few adults turned around as Ricki, coughing from the strain, stumbled toward them.

The story of the accident had already made the rounds, and within minutes several people had gathered around Ricki to hear the details. Most of them were simply curious; some had come to gloat.

"It's bad enough that old man Thomas supported an animal tormentor; now it seems his son isn't much better."

"The apple doesn't fall far from the tree. I hope Ricki remembers that; it might get her to climb down off her high horse."

Distracted by her concern for Doc Holliday's well-being, Ricki was only dimly aware of these insults. She was puzzled. What had she done to deserve this treatment? But she had no time to waste looking for an answer.

"Please," she stammered. "Please, I need a trailer."

"Then buy one," a complaining voice said insultingly.

Ricki closed her eyes for a moment, exhausted. "A double trailer. We have to load Diablo on and drive to Lillian. Holli can't go any farther, and without Diablo, he probably won't get into the trailer—"

"What kind of horse is it that won't get into a trailer alone?" the same voice continued.

Ricki felt panic rise within her. *Don't these people understand?*

"You mean to tell me there isn't one among you so-called riders willing to move his butt and help these two girls? And Doc Holliday? And you call yourselves horse lovers." Jake's voice was dripping with contempt.

He made his way to Ricki and put his arms around her shoulders. He was even paler than he had been in the last few weeks. And his breathing was labored. "So, how about it?" His eyes gleamed angrily.

Two riders, Peter and Karen, separated themselves from the group and nodded to Ricki. "Okay, then. Go get Diablo. Let's see if we can bring Lillian's horse back home."

Grateful, Ricki smiled at the two of them, and the anger that clouded Jake's face disappeared.

"What do you know? It's possible after all. I was beginning to think that this riding club was made up of nothing but self-absorbed hypocrites. I'll call Doctor Hofer and ask him to come over. By the time he arrives, you'll probably be back, too," he said, looking at Ricki.

Slowly he moved away, and Ricki ran down the corridor to get Diablo out of his stall.

*

When Diablo recognized her, he greeted her with a snort. And when Ricki examined her horse, she saw that Jake's skill at grooming had produced a true masterpiece. There were no traces of the strenuous ride visible on the horse, and his coat shone like silk.

"Come on, boy, we have to go get your friend," said Ricki. She fastened the lead onto Diablo's halter and then led him quickly out of the stall. Diablo seemed a little surprised when Ricki led him outside without a saddle. What did this all mean?

He looked at the strange horse trailer with suspicion. But when Ricki got up on the ramp in front of him, he didn't hesitate to follow her. He allowed her to tie him down. Only when Ricki slipped out the door at the front, and Peter clapped the ramp closed, did he whinny nervously.

Ricki knocked against the wall and called comfortingly,

94

"It's okay, Diablo. I'm here. Stay calm! We'll be back home soon!" Then she and the two adults got into the cab of the trailer.

"Straight ahead, then turn right toward the old railroad tracks," she explained, then she closed her eyes for a moment. "If only Holli will go into the trailer, if only Doctor Hofer doesn't find a broken bone, and if only Kevin gets better soon—if, if, if."

Without thinking, Ricki put her hand in her jacket pocket and felt the headband that she had found on the meadow.

Where have I seen this before? The question pounded again and again in her brain. Somehow, she sensed there was a connection between the ribbon and the bolting of the horses, as well as with the unknown rider who was making her life so miserable.

"There they are, in front of us!" Excitedly, Ricki looked out of the window and saw that Lillian had gone perhaps 30 more feet from the spot where she had left them both standing.

Peter allowed the car to slowly come to a stop.

Doc Holliday laid his ears back as soon as the trailer came into view. Lillian's face was like stone, but her eyes spoke volumes. It would be a fight to load Holli, even if they got him in.

Peter lowered the ramp, while Diablo whinnied continuously. Holli perked up his ears and gave a loud reply, but he wouldn't budge.

Ricki untied Diablo and led him slowly backward out of the trailer. He was obviously glad to have solid ground under his feet again, and he was happy to see Holli.

He ran straight to Doc Holliday, dragging Ricki with him, and buried his nose in his companion's mane affectionately. Holli's eyes became calmer now that his fellow horse was standing beside him.

"Let's give him a minute before we try it," said Karen. She got two poles out of the trunk and tied them to the poles in the trailer to help, if necessary, in loading the horse.

"Let's go," barked Peter, looking impatiently at his watch. If it went quickly, he could still be back in time for his jumping lesson.

But Holli wasn't interested in keeping time, and couldn't be coaxed into the trailer. He limped behind Diablo up to the ramp, but then he decided not to take one more step.

Diablo was loaded on and off several times, but Doc Holliday remained stubborn, and the more Lillian pulled on his snaffle, the more aggressive he became.

"This isn't going to work," Peter said angrily, and Lillian glowered at Ricki. "I said he wouldn't go in, right from the beginning!"

"What? You knew that?" Karen looked at Ricki with annoyance. "We could have saved ourselves a whole lot of trouble!"

Ricki rolled her eyes. "But how are we to get the horse home, if not in a trailer? Are we supposed to carry him?"

Peter made a face. "That's your problem, not ours!"

Ricki could have cried she was so mad. Once again, she asked herself what she could have done to make all the riders dislike her. Was it a crime to own Diablo? Were they all envious of her happiness with her horse?

She knew she would have to find the answers to these questions, but now was not the time. "Please," she said. "Let's try once more." Peter shrugged indifferently and turned away. Even Karen just shook her head.

"Go ahead. But it won't work!" Lillian said grimly.

96

Ricki looked at Lillian, who also appeared to have given up.

"Let's try something different," whispered Ricki. "I saw this once in a film. It worked then."

Peter snickered. "Are we dealing with normal horses here or with trained film stars?" he asked sarcastically.

Ricki ignored him and began to unfasten Holli's bit.

"What are you doing?" Lillian watched, perplexed.

"Holli is in too much pain to run away, so we can take off his snaffle," Ricki explained. "With luck, he'll follow Diablo, if we don't force him. I think if he's allowed to decide for himself whether or not he enters the trailer, we have a small chance."

Lillian didn't know what she thought of this theory, but she would do almost anything if only Holli could be taken home.

Ricki took off the saddle and put it aside. Then she approached the white horse, stroked his mane, and whispered to him, "Please don't disappoint me, we don't have any other options. You'll see. It's not that bad. Do you think Diablo would go in voluntarily if it were dangerous?" Then she stepped back in order to get Diablo out of the trailer again, while Lillian put the saddle in the car.

Doc Holliday stood as still as a statue. Lillian played with the bit nervously, and Peter stood at a distance chattering with Karen. Their stiff laughter made Ricki furious. She had to lean against Diablo for a while.

"So, my little devil, show us what you can do. If anyone can persuade Holli, you can!"

The black horse looked at her with his clever eyes and blew in her hair.

"I'm going to take that as approval of my plan," said Ricki and led her horse backward again, down the ramp, before she let the lead reins hang slack. The horse stopped for a minute, and then he went straight to Holli.

Diablo stood very close to Holli and nudged him affectionately. He seemed to know exactly what this was about. He went up to Holli sideways and leaned against him, so that Holli had to take a few steps toward the trailer in order not to lose his balance.

After a few minutes Diablo went in front of the ramp and stood still. He turned his head toward his friend and whinnied loudly. *Come on,* it was supposed to mean, but Holli didn't move an inch.

Ricki moved Diablo onto the ramp, and he whinnied to Holli again. Two more steps and Diablo was again in Peter's trailer.

Ricki tied him up and admitted to herself that her plan had failed. She didn't know what else to do and was just about to go out the front door when she heard Peter say, "Do you believe that? Just look … no one will believe that!"

Ricki stretched her head up a little in order to look past Diablo and see what was happening outside.

She couldn't believe her eyes. Holli limped slowly toward the trailer and finally stepped hesitantly onto the ramp. The hollow sound under his hooves startled him, but Diablo's gentle neighs seemed to calm him. Gradually, he climbed up the ramp until he stood beside Diablo, covered in sweat.

"Close the ramp! Quick!" Peter ordered while Ricki distributed the treats she had in her pants pocket.

Lillian stuck her head into the trailer from the front door and held out a rope to Ricki. "Can you make him a halter out of that?"

"Sure. Give it to me." With nimble fingers Ricki knotted the rope around Holli's head, leaving a small piece to tie

98

him up with. Then she quickly left the trailer and joined the others in the car.

"Thank God!" she said, relieved. "I wasn't sure it would work."

Lillian was just glad that Holli was finally going home. "Thanks," she whispered quietly to Ricki without taking her eyes from the road.

"It was the least Diablo and I could do," replied Ricki just as quietly, and she pressed Lillian's hand firmly.

Chapter 7

Mrs. Thomas met Ricki's request to visit Kevin with a stern, disapproving look, but with a shrug of resignation, she let the girl into the spacious duplex apartment.

"He's upstairs, second door on the left," she announced brusquely, and left Ricki standing in the hallway. *Nice,* the girl thought. *Maybe she's just upset because of the divorce.*

"Hey," said Ricki shyly, standing in the doorway.

"Ricki! It's great to see you. Come in."

As Ricki entered the room, she noticed that Kevin, who was lying in bed, seemed a little pale. His eyes shone for a moment, but then they darkened with sadness.

"Tell me, what's with Holli? Did Lillian get him home safely? How is he? Does he—?"

"Stop, stop! Wait!" Ricki cut him off. "So many questions. I can't answer them all at once! So, I think it'll be best if I just tell you everything that happened. But first, tell me, how's your leg?"

Kevin made a face and shoved the blanket aside. "It's in a cast," he said. "The ankle is broken!"

Ricki had to laugh. "We're really a pair with our broken bones. First me with my collarbone, and now you with your ankle."

Kevin nodded. "I just hope Holli doesn't join our group. Tell me, so I can think straight again."

Ricki smiled. She was glad that she could distract Kevin a little from his worries about Lillian's horse. After all, Dr. Hofer had found only a bad tendon strain, which was very painful but would heal. Doc Holliday couldn't be ridden for the next six weeks, but Lillian was satisfied. She had imagined the worst possible diagnosis that the vet would tell her.

Kevin breathed a sigh of relief. "Thank God! If I've learned one thing from this experience it's that I will never ride a strange horse again. I would never have gotten over it if something really serious had happened to Holli."

Ricki knew Kevin felt terrible about his part in Holli's injury and was afraid he'd stop riding again because of it. "Well, I'm glad that Diablo isn't a strange horse for you. He told me to say hello for him and that he's looking forward to practicing that jump again, when you're better."

Kevin looked skeptical. "I'm not sure I'm going to do that. I'm beginning to feel that I bring bad luck to the horses that I ride. Think about it. First Leonardo, now Holli—"

Ricki was really mad. "Kevin … you're an idiot!" she declared spontaneously. "You're a much better rider than a lot of the others in the club. And do you know why? Because you have a heart; because for you a horse isn't a sport object, he's a friend; because you respect the horse's feelings; and because you—"

"And because I have a girlfriend like you!" he jumped in, completing Ricki's sentence.

Embarrassed, the two looked at each other, not knowing what else to say.

Ricki's heart was beating with joy. She felt like she just

had to shout out her happiness, but she couldn't do that in Kevin's room. Suddenly she stood up.

"May I come back?" she asked, taking his hand in hers and giving it a good-bye squeeze.

Kevin beamed. "I hope very much that you come back. After all, I tutor you in math… ."

"Just because of math?"

Kevin looked at her tenderly. "No. Definitely not just because of math."

Ricki smiled, feeling a tingle spread throughout her whole body, as she walked toward the door. "Well, see you!"

"Till tomorrow. I'm looking forward to seeing you again. And, Ricki … thanks."

Kevin waved at her, then he closed his eyes, tired but happy.

*

The following days at the stable were horrible for Ricki. Most of the riders gave her dirty looks or just ignored her when she tried to start a conversation.

Lillian still said hello to her, but she was very standoffish since Holli's accident. Many times Ricki stood in Diablo's stall alone and realized, sadly, that she didn't understand the world anymore.

The only one who treated Ricki normally and was still friendly was Jake, who was united with her in their love for Diablo. He came to dinner or to visit the Sulais more often now. Ricki noticed that he seemed to be feeling better too.

At school Lark and Cathy had managed somehow to get most of their classmates to ignore her as well. Even Kevin noticed it.

"You can't do anything with him ever since he's been

102

hanging out with that bimbo," complained Rob, and Sean nodded his head in agreement.

"How can you understand someone like that? First you can't talk to him because of what happened to his horse, then he gets mad every time someone even uses the word 'riding,' and now he talks nonstop about it, has no time for soccer, and just hangs out with Ricki and her stupid horse. It's pathetic! Is Kevin so blind that he can't see she's just using him? Carrying her schoolbag, tutoring her in math. Well, let's see if she carries *his* bag now."

Rob grinned. "Crutches or no crutches, if that works I'm getting myself a girlfriend to carry my bag too!"

"Another girl as weird as Ricki doesn't exist," said Sean, a little louder than he had planned, with a sideways glance at Lark, who was snickering. But when Ricki and Kevin entered the classroom a little later, and he saw how caringly she pushed the chair in place for her boyfriend, put his crutches aside, and genuine showed concern, Sean felt guilty. He had to admit, he was a little envious of the obvious affection Kevin and Ricki showed each other

Ricki isn't a bimbo, he thought, and was ashamed that he hadn't owned up to his true feelings. But he'd seen firsthand how quickly his classmates could shun someone, and he certainly didn't want to risk that. As a newcomer he had his own trouble making friends. He had just recently earned his acceptance by—let's say, as a test of courage— stealing the money out of the class fund without being seen, and putting it back. He managed to do it even though Mr. Bradford guarded the petty-cash box with an eagle eye.

After this deed, Lark had selected Sean to be her personal accomplice, and this gave him, a former outsider, a higher rank in the class hierarchy, where Lark had taken control.

In order to maintain his standing with his classmates,

Sean had to perform the nasty little pranks against Lark's former friend. Lately, he had been thinking about having an open and honest conversation with Kevin and Ricki, but he was afraid that afterward the others wouldn't talk to him again. However, his conscience was beginning to bother him, and he didn't know how long he would be able to take the pressure.

*

"I can't stand this much longer," Ricki exploded one day at dinner.

"What can't you stand much longer?" Brigitte Sulai turned to her daughter questioningly. "Do I cook that bad?"

"Oh, Mom, it's not your cooking!" Ricki assured her, while she toyed with the food on her plate. "I just don't know what to do anymore. At school no one will talk to me; at the stable, same thing. By the way, there's a rumor that money is missing there too. Lillian avoids me, and everyone looks at me as though I had bubonic plague."

She paused and stared into space before she said quietly, "That wouldn't be all that bad, but what really bothers me is that Diablo is still being ridden at night, seldom, but nevertheless—!"

Hearing her daughter's list of problems, Brigitte turned serious. "Slowly, one thing at a time. The only way you will be able to do anything about school is to have a talk with your classmates."

"Ha! How? They turn around and leave if I so much as take a breath!"

"Then a teacher will have to take part too."

"I don't want that, and anyway, a teacher can't help me at the stable."

"Yeah, what's going on there? Are they saying you're responsible for the theft?"

Ricki shrugged. "Not openly, but there are rumors, and I think Lark and Cathy have spread them around the school."

Ricki's mother became really furious and struck the table with her fist. The glasses, which were full of water, began to wobble.

"That's it! This has been going on for way too long. Do you know what I'm going to do? I'm going to call the parents of your so-called girlfriends and have a serious conversation with them. I should have done it a lot sooner."

Startled, Ricki looked up. "Please, Mom, don't do that! I think everything would just get worse. And you said that you have to be very careful with accusations."

"Yes, that's true, but I just can't let these silly teenage problems go on any longer. It's getting ridiculous now."

"But, Mom—" Ricki tried to counter, but Brigitte waved that away.

"About Diablo. Which days do you think he is being ridden?"

Ricki looked up at the ceiling. She didn't know. "I have no idea, it depends; but I think that he's being ridden two, maybe three times a month."

"But no particular days?"

Ricki shook her head. "No, it's always different."

"There's no regular pattern, which makes it more difficult of course."

For a while both mother and daughter were lost in their thoughts, and then Brigitte made a decision.

"We're going to watch the stalls at night, at different times. Maybe we'll be lucky and catch the rider in the act."

Ricki jumped up and threw her arms around her mother's neck. She would never have expected her to react like

105

this. Finally, she wouldn't have to just stand by and do nothing. She was glad that the uncertainty about Diablo's night rides would soon be over, but she dreaded finding out who was doing this behind her back.

"It's time for you to have a little peace," said Brigitte softly, and gave Ricki a hug.

Ricki enjoyed her mother's embrace, but a troubling thought made her pull away. "Mom, please don't call Lark and Cathy's parents. I suspect it's them, but if it's not, then everything will just get worse."

Ricki's mother turned her head back and forth pondering her daughters request, "Maybe you're right. We'll wait to see what happens. The telephone isn't going anywhere."

"Thanks, Mom." Ricki felt relieved. After all, she didn't want anymore trouble than she already had.

*

"Hey, it's great that your parents are finally going to do something," said Kevin when Ricki told him about the plan. "It's just too bad I can't be there when you catch this jerk!"

"We don't have him yet," said Ricki, who, having kicked off her shoes, was sitting on the edge of his bed with her knees pulled up. She wiggled her toes back and forth, and pointed at his cast.

"When are you getting that thing off?"

"Tomorrow I'm getting a walking cast, but I still won't be able to do much."

"Hmmm," said Ricki, and Kevin noticed that his girl-friend was thinking about something completely different, despite her question. But he could understand that.

Gently, he poked her. "Hey, you! Don't worry about me.

106

See to it that you get to Diablo and teach him to speak, so that he can finally tell us who's been riding him."

Ricki laughed. She leaned in and looked lovingly at him. "I'm so glad that you exist," she said quietly, and Kevin took her head in his hands and drew her toward him.

"I love you," he whispered just before he gave her an awkward but very gentle kiss on the lips.

*

Diablo had stretched his head far over the edge of the stall and was looking for Ricki, as he did every day. He seemed to have an inner clock that told him when she would be coming around the corner to see him.

Today, however, she was a little later than usual, and the horse was kicking against the stall door with his hooves, in a bad mood.

Lillian, who had already brushed Holli and now stood in the corridor, glanced at Diablo, who was making more and more noise.

She had to smile. He was so much like her own horse, who would pace back and forth in his stall until he finally got to see his owner and then whinny a loud greeting.

Lillian went to Diablo's stall and stroked him across his nose. "Did she forget you today? Calm down a little bit. She'll be here soon."

As Ricki came running into the stable out of breath, Lillian, not wanting Ricki to see her near Diablo, quickly disappeared from in front of his stall. He only had eyes for his owner anyway.

"Come, my sweetie! I'm sorry I made you wait today. Kevin says to tell you hello, and that he is going to visit you next week with an extra large carrot."

Lillian jerked as she heard Kevin's name. She was still furious about what had happened to her beloved Doc Holliday when Kevin was riding him. She was standing with her back to Ricki, nonchalantly looking out the window.

Ricki had given up trying to have a conversation with her. Every time she tried, she'd been rejected, and that hurt.

Diablo was content again. He had been greeted by Ricki's caresses and a delicious apple. Ricki went to get her grooming basket, which she had left on the bench underneath the riding schedule. On the way, she stopped at Doc Holliday's stall. She held a carrot out to him and looked at him with affection.

"Hello, little one, how are you today? Are you still in pain? You can't believe how sorry I am for the whole thing."

"And how sorry *I* am!" Lillian's voice was bitter.

Ricki turned around quickly. She hadn't heard Lillian approaching her. At that same moment, she remembered the words of her mother, "You have to try to talk with her to clear things up." So she took a deep breath and decided to try once more to set things straight with Lillian.

"Let's talk, please," she began cautiously. But Holli's owner just raised both hands.

"Thanks—not interested!"

"But—"

"No buts! I don't want to! Don't you get it?"

Lillian turned around and wanted to leave, but Ricki was tired of being the one who had to beg all the time. Furious, she stamped the ground with her foot.

"But I want to talk with you, and that's what I'm going to do, whether you like it or not, whether you listen or not! Whether I have to keep running after you forever or not, I'm going to say what's on my mind, and I'm not going to

108

beg you to listen, you just won't have any choice! Do you understand?"

Lillian turned pale at Ricki's aggressive tone. Finally realizing there was no sense in running away and closing her ears, she gave a single nod of consent.

Several riders who were grooming their horses in the stalls became very quiet all of a sudden. They didn't want to miss anything that might be said.

"Let's talk somewhere else," said Lillian softly, but Ricki stood her ground and said loudly, "Why? Anyone can hear what I have to say!"

"But not what I have to say to you."

"Huh?" Ricki looked a little confused as Lillian walked past her and hurried down the corridor toward the stairs that led to the riders' lounge.

Ricki followed her more slowly and could hear giggling and a sneering voice say, "Now they'll tear each other apart."

She sensed an enormous rage rising within her that was hard to control. She entered the riders' lounge and shut the door behind her.

Lillian was seated on the bench in front of the old wood-burning stove, resigned to the conversation to come.

"Good—who goes first?" she asked, visibly tense.

Ricki was also nervous. She had wanted to talk with Lillian for so long, and now she didn't know how to begin.

"You begin," she said in a shaking voice, hoping that it would be easier for her to express her own feelings after she'd heard what Lillian had to say.

"Okay—where should I begin?" Lillian seemed to have the same problems with getting started. "It isn't so easy. You can't imagine how upset I was when the accident with Holli happened." She paused briefly.

109

"Yes, I can, I—" began Ricki. But she was interrupted immediately.

"Please, don't say anything! I know you can understand my reaction, especially now that you have your own horse. Holli and I have been together now for about five years, and I've always made sure that he is well taken care of and stays healthy and all that. If I hadn't made you guys that stupid offer, he could be standing in his stall now, completely healthy and pain free. That means I blame myself for this accident, not you or Kevin. I should have realized that something could happen in that moment when I gave my responsibility for Holli over to you," Lillian admitted, nervously fingering the beads on her thin leather bracelet.

"After all, you can only take care of your horse when you are near him. Of course, anything can happen anytime, but I keep asking myself, 'What if I kept my mouth shut?' But I can't change anything and it hurts me that Holli is hurt, do you understand? A dumb question. Of course you do! I saw how you suffered with Diablo when he was being mistreated."

Lillian got up and walked to the window and stared out at the huge ancient tree on the front lawn.

"You know, there are things that aren't easy to explain … feelings that can hardly be expressed in words. I can still see you both on that afternoon," she said, turning back to look at Ricki. "You two were so happy and so in love and I was happy for you. That was the reason that I gave Kevin Holli for that ride.

"And then, after the accident, I was so worried about my horse, that maybe he would never walk right again—or maybe something even worse—and my feelings just took over. I really hated you two … hated you because of Holli's

110

pain … hated you because of my fear … hated you for my helplessness … and hated you for my irresponsibility toward Holli. I can't tell you how glad I was to see Kevin lying on the ground with his broken ankle. Serves him right, I thought. He should suffer exactly as much as Holli!"

Lillian sniffed back tears before continuing. "And then somehow I realized that it wasn't your fault at all. It was my fault entirely. First of all, I could have ridden Holli; second, a horse can stumble at any time; and third, I have known for some time that Holli bolts on that meadow, and I should have told you two. And finally, after I had realized all this, I was just angry with myself and didn't want to lose face with you, if I'm honest. That's why I was always so distant to you. And there's something else that you should know …"

Lillian came back to the bench and sat across from Ricki, who hardly moved a muscle in all that time. She hardly dared to breathe. She felt compassion for her friend, who wasn't having an easy time telling her this. She listened closely as Lillian continued.

"Actually, I should be grateful to you two for riding across that meadow. Don't think this is easy for me to say, but considering that Holli doesn't have any serious injuries and has to rest for only for a brief time before he can run again without any pain, I can talk about being grateful. But I don't want you to tell anyone what I am going to tell you now. Do you hear me? You have to promise not to tell anyone even one word of it."

Ricki nodded and bent over a little because Lillian was almost whispering.

"You can say I'm crazy, and that's the reason that I don't want anyone to find out anything! To be honest, I'm almost glad that Holli is now standing in his stall with a bandaged

111

leg, at peace. For a long time now, I've had the feeling that every once in a while someone—I have no idea who—has been secretly riding Holli. He has changed so much. He doesn't react to my gestures as well as he used to and sometimes he's really tired before I even start my ride. And what's most important, he bolts at the same spots on the trail, something he never did before."

"What? Holli too?" Ricki couldn't restrain herself longer. "That's unbelievable!"

Lillian was startled. "What do you mean, 'too'?" she asked.

"What do you think? 'Too' means 'too'!"

"What? Diablo—?"

Ricki nodded forcefully. "Exactly! We noticed it because of how tired he has been and the saddle equipment. It was on the wrong rack, although I had put it on the right one. Also, he bolted with me on the same meadow, too, for the first time!"

"No!" Now it was Lillian's turn to sit there with her mouth open. "And? Did you do anything about it?"

"No, of course not! What could I do? After all, you just said it yourself. Everyone would probably just have laughed at my suspicions. But I'm hopeful that I'll catch the ghost rider. My mother and I have decided to observe the stalls at irregular times at night. Maybe we'll get lucky."

For a moment both girls were silent and just looked at each other knowingly. Each tried to guess the thoughts of the other.

"I'm sorry," said Ricki all of a sudden.

Lillian slowly nodded her head. "I know. I'm sorry too." Then she smiled and reached out her hand to Ricki. "Friends?" she asked.

"Friends!" answered Ricki, and they hugged each other relieved and happy that they had cleared everything up between them.

"Oh," Lillian hit her head with her hand. "I just thought of something! You want to observe the stalls? Maybe I can give you a tip. I have noticed that Holli is usually ridden on days when the moon is bright. A few weeks ago, he was being ridden more often than lately. Someone picked out the bright nights on purpose for his rides, so that he didn't have to ride in the dark."

Ricki thought it over. "You might be right. Maybe, or probably, both of our horses were ridden together. So, there could be two mystery riders we have to catch! And I just remembered, there were deep hoof tracks in the meadow where Diablo and Holli bolted, as if a race had taken place on the wet ground. And on the way back, I found a red-and-white-striped headband. You can believe me or not, but I'm sure I've seen it somewhere before."

"That would mean that we might know these night riders."

"Exactly!"

The girls sat silently thinking about the situation. Then Ricki got up slowly and a little stiffly.

"Well, let's hope we know more soon. What do you say? Are we okay? Is everything cleared up between us? I should go look after Diablo."

Lillian smiled. "Are you going riding?"

"Yeah, I think so. Do you want to? You shouldn't get out of practice while Holli is healing."

Lillian stopped short. Then she laughed.

"Sure, why not? But don't make a scene if Diablo stumbles!"

"I promise!"

113

The two girls happily left the riders' lounge together arm in arm. Ricki wanted to get the saddle equipment first and disappeared into the tack room, and Lillian went straight to the horses.

"Well? How did it go? Did you make her feel like an idiot?" a few curious voices wanted to know.

"Of course! And now I'm going to ride her Diablo until he's exhausted!" Then, leaving several riders standing with their mouths hanging open, she ran into the stall of the black horse to explain to him that today he was going to have another rider in addition to Ricki.

*

Lillian had ridden Diablo for a half-hour in the ring. When she dismounted, she was more than just enthusiastic.

"He's amazing! Do you know what I think, Ricki? The two of us have the two best horses in the world! Thanks for letting me ride. It was really, really super, but now you ride. I have to devote some time to my invalid."

Ricki's heart swelled with pride, and she glanced at her watch when she had the reins in her hand. "It's just 4 p.m. I think I'll go outside for an hour. The weather is so nice and warm today. I have to take advantage of it."

"Sure! Be careful and avoid the racing path. We don't want anything to happen to you. Two invalids are enough!" Lillian called after her. Ricki swung herself up into the saddle in the parking lot of the riding academy. She waved happily to her friend.

As Diablo distanced himself from the stable with long steps, Ricki took a deep breath and closed her eyes for a moment. She was incredibly happy right now. Life seemed so easy, as though she were floating, without problems and worries, and she gave herself up to Diablo's rhythm. She could ride like this forever. The horse carried her through a small path of woods, where the light of the evening sun shone through the trees. Three deer stood in a clearing and ate, undisturbed by Diablo and his rider. For a few moments, Ricki and Diablo remained still, listening to the sounds of nature. She could have embraced the whole world. She increased the pressure of her thighs a little, and the black horse started to gallop from a standstill.

When Ricki returned to the stable, she noticed that something had changed deep within her. Life had communicated to her the meaning of her existence. She no longer felt any hate or rage for those who were making her life difficult. Quite the contrary. Her heart opened up to let herself feel compassion and understanding for those who seemed only capable of sowing unrest and jealousy.

"Actually, these people are to be pitied," she said softly to Diablo while she unsaddled him. "They don't know how wonderful life can be. Why waste it plotting against harmless people?"

Diablo just looked at her with his clever eyes and rubbed his head on her shoulder. For him, life with Ricki had really begun, and he had decided to do his part to make them both happy.

Chapter 8

"Ricki! Ricki! Get up!" Quietly, but insistently, Brigitte whispered in her daughter's ear.

"Oh, Mom, I don't have to be at school today until the second period," Ricki grumbled, pulling the blanket over her head and turning to the other side.

"I'm not waking you up to go to school. It's the middle of the night. Don't you remember? I thought we were going to Diablo's stall?"

That worked! Ricki shot up in bed. "Oh, yeah! Of course! I'll be ready right away!" She jumped out of bed and put on the clothes she had laid out for herself earlier that night.

"Put on another sweater; it's pretty cold out there!"

Ricki nodded. She was freezing anyway from being torn out of her warm bed so abruptly. She ran down the stairs behind her mother, her teeth clattering with the cold. She grabbed an apple out of the blue glass bowl on the hall table and together they left the house on tiptoe.

Brigitte Sulai let the car roll out of the driveway quietly before stepping on the gas and turning toward the riding academy. Music was playing softly on the radio, and it was enough to lull Ricki back to sleep. Only the thought of Diablo kept her awake. She imagined what she and her mother would do if they actually confronted the mystery riders, especially if those unknown riders were strong, or even brutal, men. That thought upset Ricki, but then she remembered that her horse still had a sweet disposition. So the ghost riders can't be bad people at heart, even if they did take the horses out of their stalls at night and ride them without permission.

Just a minute, she thought, with a sudden flash of self-awareness. *Remember what you almost did: You planned to kidnap Diablo to prevent him from being sold. So to be honest with yourself, you have to admit that you're not much different from the ghost riders.*

"Are you sleeping again?" Brigitte asked, surprised at how silent her daughter was. Normally she was very talkative.

"Not yet, but if the music doesn't change, I will be!"

"Don't you think it's funny that my choice of music puts you to sleep, while yours won't let me sleep?" Brigitte parried playfully, just before she turned down the narrow dirt road that led directly to the riding academy.

"Up ahead there's a fork," directed Ricki. "You could stop there. When the lights are out no one can see the car behind the bushes."

Brigitte nodded and slowly turned right. Having driven to the stable only a few times, she felt a little unsure of this stretch of road. But Ricki, on the other hand, who was here with Diablo almost every day, could have found anything within a two-mile radius blindfolded.

After they had parked the car, mother and daughter armed themselves with flashlights and walked the rest of the way to the stable. It was pitch black and all was still around the building. Jake's apartment was dark as well.

"Everything's quiet. No one seems to be about tonight," whispered Brigitte, and Ricki nodded in agreement.

"I'm going to creep over to the entrance door to see if it's locked. Wait here. If the door is open, I will signal you with my flashlight. Otherwise, I'll be right back."

Ricki felt her way to the door. She was scared to death, but she would never have admitted that to her mother. She kept going courageously until she was standing in front of the heavy wooden door.

Okay, she thought. *Don't have a breakdown now,* she pleaded with herself as she took a deep breath and carefully tried to turn the knob. But the door was locked. Ricki was relieved, but she knew that now the same buildup of stress would happen again tomorrow night.

"Nothing!" she said when she was back with her mother.

"That's okay with me," Brigitte answered, and together they ran back to the car. The digital clock beside the steering wheel indicated that it was 2:07 in the morning.

"I can't imagine that they would ride even later than that—unless they don't have to go to work or to school."

A bit perplexed, Brigitte turned to her daughter while she started the car's engine.

"What do you mean 'they'? How many riders can fit onto Diablo's saddle?"

Only then did Ricki realize that she had been including the ghost rider that was riding Lillian's horse. At first she didn't want to say anything, but then she decided that her mother had a right to know in spite of her promise to Lillian not to tell anyone.

"Oh, *that's* what's happening," said Brigitte after Ricki finished telling her about Lillian's suspicions. By then they were almost back home. "Maybe we should tell the police after all, if it's happening to other horse owners and people are borrowing any horse at any time of the night."

Ricki was too tired to answer. She couldn't wait to go

118

back to bed, and was glad when her mother unlocked the front door. As they stood in the hallway taking off their jackets, Ricki leaned against her mother's shoulder and smiled with eyes closed.

"Thanks, Mom. I am sooo tired."

"Well, then, get to bed! In four hours you have to get up and go to school!" Brigitte said, giving Ricki a quick hug and a gentle push in the direction of the stairs.

"Oh, God, school. I forgot all about it. Couldn't it be that we have a day off or a school break? Or maybe it's a weekend?"

Brigitte laughed quietly. "Get going—and sleep tight!"

"Good night." Ricki couldn't even remember how she had found her bed. But she was asleep as soon as her head touched the pillow.

*

The next day, in spite of her early-morning adventure, Ricki was wide awake at school and able to concentrate on her work better than ever before.

After stopping off at home for her after-school snack and short visit with her mother and Harry, she got on her bike, as she did every day, and rode to the stable to see Diablo. As she turned into the parking lot of the riding academy, she noticed a big black limousine. While Ricki was busy parking her bike along the wall of the building, two men, whom she didn't recognize, left the stable talking.

"You can't see anything that would make you believe that that horse had been mistreated. It's a beauty," one of the men said.

"Yeah, but we should try to find the young girl before someone else does. What was her name? Ricki? She should be easy to find. Actually, it's strange that there wasn't anyone in the stalls now, don't you agree?"

"Yeah, but be glad. If no one is there, then no one can ask any questions. I hate to be hounded with questions when people find out why we are at a certain location!"

Laughing, the two men walked back to their car while Ricki was cautiously watching them from around the corner of the building. Overhearing their conversation, she had been both curious and afraid at the same time, but she hadn't found the courage to introduce herself to the two men. Who knows, maybe there was some connection between them and the nighttime rides?

When she heard the car drive away, she slipped into the stable, retrieved her grooming basket, and breathed a sigh of relief when Diablo whinnied cheerfully at her as she approached his stall.

"If only you could speak," she sighed, as she started to brush him till his coat shone.

*

"One thing I can tell you. You're not going to get up every night and chase after imaginary midnight riders."

Marcus Sulai looked at his daughter with disapproval and she looked at him in disbelief.

"But Dad, those two men—"

"They were at the stable while it was still daylight. You don't think they were planning something bad, do you? If they were, they would have come in the middle of the night!"

Ricki was desperate. Why couldn't her father understand her worries about her horse?

"Mom, say something!" The girl looked pleadingly at her mother, who had been listening to the conversation silently.

"Well," she said hesitantly, "we can't keep doing these nightly tours forever… ."

"But we only did it once!"

"Yeah, I know, but in the long run?"

"I have a great book." Harry joined the conversation suddenly. "*Detective Socks Saves the Black Stallion*."

"Yeah, and—?" Ricki interrupted her little brother. "Don't you think we have better things to do than have a stupid book discussion?"

Harry rolled his eyes. "You guys haven't been listening," he said with an insulted look on his face. "Detective Socks is a little boy who is able to prevent the theft of a horse because he locks himself into the stall at night. He was in the stall about a hundred times before they caught the thief."

"How often? A hundred times? Are you crazy?"

"Ricki! Don't take your frustration out on your brother!" Brigitte scolded her eldest child.

"Excuse me!" replied Ricki in exasperation. "But 100 days is ridiculous!"

Harry was very serious. "Well, maybe it wasn't exactly one hundred, but it was at least three!"

"Well, I suggest the following," Marcus offered. "Tomorrow morning I'll call the police. We probably should have done that much sooner." Marcus looked at each one gravely. "Whether they do something about it is another matter. Usually they don't do anything until something bad happens."

"Great! Really fabulous!" Ricki was outraged. "That means I get to stand by twiddling my thumbs while my horse continues to be ridden at night by an unknown rider.

Terrific! Super! I'm ecstatic! Oh, man, this is driving me crazy!"

She jumped up and ran out of the kitchen, slamming the door behind her. Her parents exchanged concerned looks. Even Harry recognized how serious the situation was and wisely decided to remain silent.

Ricki had grabbed the cell phone as she ran out, and now she lay on her bed, fuming. She dialed Kevin's number with shaking hands and closed her eyes, relieved when she heard his voice.

"Kevin? This is Ricki. Things are getting critical!"

*

"What a shame one of the horses is lame. Now only one of us can ride."

Whispering, two dark figures cautiously approached the riding academy. The moonlight had illuminated the area enough so that one could just make them out.

"Nonsense! You know what? Let's both ride the black one together."

"We've never done that before!"

"Well then, it's time we did!"

In the distance they could hear the church tower clock strike 1:30 a.m.

"We're early today," one of the mysterious figures said.

"Yeah, but the old grouch seems to be asleep already anyway. Lucky for us that he's a bit hard of hearing," the other one added.

Carefully, they crept on. They made a large curve around the riding academy and disappeared into the darkness.

A short time later, the soft light of a lamp that had been

covered could be seen behind one of the windows in the stable.

*

Groaning, Jake turned from one side to the other. He had gone to bed early this evening, after he had conscientiously locked the entrance to the riding academy and made an inspection of the stalls.

The stable master was glad when it was time to quit this evening. He hadn't been feeling well all day and it had been a huge effort for him to finish his work. He had a hard time walking, and his breathing was so labored it felt like a ton of oats was lying on his chest. The pain in the upper middle of his chest had come back, and his heart seemed to be clamped in an iron ring. He felt panic stricken and claustrophobic, and it made him sick and terribly afraid.

With trembling hands, he wiped the sweat from his forehead and felt for the lamp on his nightstand. Breathing heavily, he switched on the lamp and glanced at his alarm clock: 1:43 a.m.

My God, thought Jake. *How will I survive this night?*

Now that the light had illuminated the room the old man felt a little better.

Light means life, went through his mind. *And I want to live. For Diablo!* But at the same time, he realized that Diablo would do just fine without him. After all, now there was Ricki to take care of him. Oh, yes, Ricki. What had she been telling him? Jake tried to distract himself from the pain by concentrating on the conversation Ricki and Kevin had had with him a while ago. He tried to remember each word but his memory failed him.

"It's awful to get old," he complained to himself aloud. "You forget everything!"

He began to get upset, and the more upset he got, the worse the pain in his chest became.

He got up grunting, and he pressed his hands over his heart. *This isn't going to end well!* he thought, frightened. *I need help, otherwise it's all over.* With the greatest effort, the old man got out of bed and wobbled the few steps to his bureau, where he kept his telephone.

He seldom used the phone. Whom should he call? Trembling, he searched through the drawer. Where was the card with the emergency numbers? He went through pictures of horses and scraps of paper with all sorts of notes until he finally found the little blue card. On it, under the printed numbers of the EMS and the fire and police departments, Ricki had written down her telephone number—just in case anything should go wrong with Diablo, Jake could call her immediately.

He looked at the numbers, hesitating. He didn't want to call the EMS, and he wasn't sure he should call the Sulais this late at night. But then the pain in his chest got worse, and he picked up the receiver and tapped in Ricki's number. He was relieved to hear a sleepy voice answer after the sixth ring.

"Sulai residence. What? Jake, is that you? What's wrong? It's very late! Is anything wrong with Diablo?"

Ricki was wide awake immediately. Since her room was the closest to the upstairs extension phone, she was the one who had answered it. The rest of the family came stumbling into the hallway, having been awakened by the phone as well. They all looked at Ricki expectantly.

Ricki had turned very pale. "It's Jake, Dad. He's really sick. He—"

Marcus took the receiver from her in an instant. "Jake? What's wrong? Stay calm, I'll be there right away, and then I'll take you to the hospital. Better yet, I'll call the EMS now. See you soon."

He pressed down on the receiver button and as soon as the line was free, he called 911.

Ricki has only heard the first few words of the conversation, and then she disappeared. Two minutes later she was fully dressed and ready.

Marcus had dressed quickly and told Brigitte, Harry, and Ricki to go back to bed. He was going to drive to Jake's alone.

"I'm going with you!" said Ricki with a determined voice.

Since there was no time to discuss it, Marcus accepted his daughter's offer without a word.

While the two of them hurried to the garage, Brigitte took her young son back to bed.

"Will Grandpa Jake die?" asked a frightened Harry, as his mother tucked the blankets around him. But Brigitte could only shrug her shoulders.

"I don't know, but let's try to believe that he will soon be better."

She lay down beside the little boy to comfort him until he went back to sleep, while she herself felt the pain of her sadness. Everyone in the family had grown to love Jake.

*

"Can't you be careful? You're making enough noise for 10 people!" a furious voice hissed along the corridor.

"What can I do when the old idiot leaves the wheelbarrow in the middle of the corridor with all the pitchforks in it?" came the answer, accompanied by a painful groan.

Carefully, the two intruders continued walking along the stable corridor, while the horses began to stomp restlessly and whinny their displeasure at the unusually loud noise at this time of night.

"Today just isn't our day! Maybe we should disappear!"

"No way! Now that we're here, we're going to ride. Do you think I came here for nothing? I'm going to saddle him now, and you can get the key out of the riders' lounge. You know, behind the counter, the second drawer from the bottom."

"Yeah, yeah. Where else would it be? This hiding place isn't very original, but that's typical for Jake. He was never very good at thinking."

"Don't talk so much. Hurry up—the night is short!"

The two shadows separated, and while one hurried to Diablo with the saddle equipment, the other crept silently up to the riders' lounge. A strange feeling of unrest began to bother the late-night visitor, and although the two had come and gone in the night often in the last few weeks, tonight was different. Something was in the air. It was unexplainable, but nevertheless, the mysterious visitor felt it.

Silently the shadow pressed along the wall in the gallery, slipped through the door, and reached confidently for the key in the drawer behind the riders' bar. Quickly the mysterious burglar started back down, but hadn't yet reached the bottom when the door to Jake's apartment, which was on the other side above the stalls, opened.

"Oh, damn!" cursed the unknown figure, who, startled, dropped the key and ran noisily the rest of the way down the stairs.

"What's going on? Hey, you—stand still! What are you doing?" Jake stood in the doorway to his room, holding on tightly to the doorframe, breathing heavily. Finally he was able to stumble over to the riders' lounge. He wanted to get the key, so that he could open the door for Marcus and the EMS doctor. But he was upset to discover that the drawer was empty.

"My God," he mumbled, becoming sicker and sicker.He was becoming weaker by the minute but pushed himself to move forward and down the wooden stairs to get to the stable corridor. Before he had reached the light switch, he heard two voices and the *clop, clop* of hooves on the cement floor.

"Let's go! Jake is coming! Let's get out of here!"

"But Diablo—"

"Let him be! C'mon—c'mon!"

There seemed to be a brief struggle, then Jake heard someone stumble and yell, "The lamp! Damn it, the lamp broke!"

When Jake had finally turned on the light switch, he heard steps hurry away quickly—and then silence. Leaning on the wall for support, Jake made his way to the first stall and rested against it, exhausted and confused.

Diablo stood, saddled, in the middle of the corridor, and rolled his eyes in fear. In front of him was a broken kerosene lantern. Little tongues of flame were already spreading from the lamp to a pile of straw that Jake had spread out for the next day.

Jake, panic stricken, tried to get to the fire, but the shock and exertion were too much for his heart. In slow motion, his legs gave way and he sank, unconscious, to the floor.

"Look, Jake has turned on all the lights. He can't be that sick, then," said Marcus, relieved, as he drove into the yard in front of the riding academy. At almost the same time, the ambulance arrived with Dr. Kennedy, the EMS doctor on duty.

"Did you call?" he asked Marcus, who was quickly walking toward him as the EMS technicians were readying the gurney. Marcus nodded and introduced himself, while Ricki tried the door of the stable.

"It won't open! Jake forgot to unlock the door! Jake! Open the door—we're here!"

For a moment, all were silent.

"And now what?" asked the doctor.

"Something's wrong," Ricki mumbled and sniffed the air. "What is that? It smells funny. Don't you notice it?"

Marcus and Dr. Kennedy inhaled deeply.

"Smells like a straw fire—" said one of the EMS workers.

"Oh God!" Ricki raced around the corner to the stalls and screamed. "It's on fire! Dad! The stalls are burning! Diablo! Noooo!"

The men came running and, for just a moment, stood frozen in shock when they saw the flames lapping at the rear windows. The doctor ran back to the car immediately and called the fire station, while Marcus looked for a way to open the door to the stalls.

Ricki, who was able to peer through one of the windows the flames had not yet reached, screamed to her father, "Dad, Jake is lying on the corridor floor and Diablo is standing between him and the fire with his saddle on. Do something, they're all going to burn up—" Ricki became hysterical with fear and began to scream continually.

"Is there another entrance anywhere? Tell me, RICKI!" her father demanded.

But Ricki kept screaming, as though she were crazy, staring fixedly at her beloved horse, who was trying to protect Jake from the fire.

Dr. Kennedy shook Ricki's shoulders to get her to stop screaming, but it didn't work. Then he slapped her face lightly, twice. Completely shocked, she stared at the doctor uncomprehendingly.

"Sorry, but that was necessary!"

"Damn it, I can't get the door open and all of the windows have bars on the inside—" a frustrated Marcus growled.

In the meantime, the fire had eaten a path along the stalls and up the walls, and the fearful cries of the animals snapped Ricki back to reality. "There's one possibility of getting into the stalls, and that's through the defect in the outer wall behind the riding ring railing."

"No chance, the railing is already on fire. Damn it, where are the firemen?" Marcus looked toward the road, feeling thwarted and unable to help.

At last they could hear the sirens in the distance, but it would be a few minutes before they arrived.

"Maybe Diablo can do something from inside—" Ricki suggested hopefully.

"Sweetheart, I don't think—" Marcus began.

But Ricki was already banging her fists against the next stall window to get Diablo's attention. "Diablo—I'm here … come … please … you have to open the door. Can you hear me? Open the DOOR!"

Marcus and Dr. Kennedy exchanged skeptical glances, but Ricki kept on yelling to Diablo.

Suddenly the horse realized it was his owner's voice calling to him, and he reacted with a knowing whinny and toss of his head. Ricki kept on yelling instructions to her horse and banged on one window after another. Diablo followed her on the inside along the corridor.

"He doesn't really understand what she's saying, does he?" the doctor asked Marcus incredulously, staring in disbelief as the horse followed the calls of his owner.

129

Ricki had reached the most difficult area. Now she had to get the horse to go about 30 feet along the corridor to the main door, and there were no windows. She ran ahead and banged as loudly as she could on the door.

"I'm here, Diablo! Come, my good boy—come here!"

And Diablo came.

Ricki and Marcus banged and kicked against the heavy wooden door and heard the horse becoming more and more agitated. Suddenly they heard a heavy crash against the door from inside. The wood creaked and groaned but didn't give way.

Ricki's voice cracked as she continued to encourage Diablo.

Then a loud bang, as though something had exploded, rang through the air. Diablo panicked, reared up, and hammered at the door with his hooves—again and again—until it finally burst open under the weight of the large black gelding.

Through the splintered boards, Ricki started to calm her horse while Marcus and Dr. Kennedy pried the lock off and finally were able to open the door.

Diablo ran past them out of the stable, opening the way for Ricki, her father, and the emergency team, who ran into the corridor without hesitation.

Dr. Kennedy kneeled beside Jake, who was lying unconscious on the floor, and checked for a pulse. Then, with the help of his team, they carried him safely out of the burning building. Ricki and her father, shielding themselves with horse blankets, ran along the corridor opening one stall after another and leading the horses outside.

Ricki was happily relieved to see Holli limping along the corridor to safety.

There was another loud bang and the ceiling track lighting came crashing to the ground with sparks flying.

Marcus was just able to pull his daughter to safety in time. "We have to get out of here! There's no more time. Come on—let's go!"

Ricki used all of her strength to fend off her father's iron grip. "Bronco and Sugar are still in there! We can't let them burn to death—let me go!"

At the same moment, three firemen stormed into the corridor. "Get out immediately! The ceiling is about to fall down!" one of them ordered.

"But the horses—" Ricki started to shout, but her constant coughing and sore throat, so dry and painful from the smoke and heat, prevented her from uttering another word.

"Get out, I said!" the fireman repeated forcefully.

The fireman pushed Ricki roughly in front of him, then Marcus grabbed her by the hand and pulled her out of the blazing building.

In the meantime streams of water were flooding through the windows, which had burst from the heat. The noise of the exploding windows almost covered the desperate neighing of Bronco and Sugar.

"Noooooooo—" screamed Ricki, just before she collapsed to the ground in a faint. Calm and darkness spread through her even before the last two horses, with singed coats, were driven out of the collapsing stable.

Chapter 9

While some of the firemen were busy putting out the fire, the rest were frantically trying to catch the horses, which had fled, panic stricken, into the darkness. The piercing wail of emergency-vehicle sirens combined with the bright revolving lights of the police cars and ambulances made rounding up the horses especially difficult. But the plaintive whinnying of the terrified animals aided the rescuers in locating them, and brought them to a nearby paddock.

"Look at this one. Can someone tell me how a fully saddled horse can be here at this time of night?" asked Max Roberts, sweating profusely under his fireman's helmet. His face looked like it was about to explode.

"Lucky thing that horses are herd animals," said policeman Ray Lester, whose expression turned from relief to bewilderment when his friend Max approached the paddock with the fully saddled Diablo.

"We can't let him run loose like that. I'll take the saddle off him, and you can get me a large plastic tarp to put it and the other equipment in. It's possible that the saddled horse may have had something to do with the fire."

Max took charge of Diablo, who was stretching his neck and sniffing the air. He pranced about excitedly and looked for Jake and Ricki. But he couldn't see them in the dark and through all the smoke.

*

Jake was already in the first ambulance on the way to the hospital. Dr. Kennedy had diagnosed him as having had a heart attack and had given him first aid before the old stable master was placed onto the gurney and into the vehicle.

Jake came to for a moment and, before he sank back into unconsciousness, whispered softly, almost too softly for anyone to hear: "There were two people … I heard them. The voices … very familiar … if I only I'd known. Ricki was right. Diablo was … ridden—"

One of the policemen had written down Jake's words, and now he knelt down beside Marcus, who was supporting his daughter's back. Ricki sat on the ground with a blanket around her shoulders and had one hard coughing fit after the other.

Lupo, the stable tomcat, sat on her lap with disheveled fur and huddled closely in fear.

"Can you make anything of these word fragments?" asked Officer Clint Fox, looking at Marcus and Ricki attentively.

"We sure can," answered Marcus, hugging Ricki close. "I didn't believe it at first, when my daughter told me she suspected that her horse was being ridden secretly at night, but now—"

"Don't forget the two men," croaked Ricki.

Marcus began to tell the story. Ricki was just too tired.

The doctor examined her and recommended that she be admitted to the hospital for observation; she had inhaled a lot of smoke and might need treatment. But Ricki begged him to let her go home. Since she had regained full consciousness quickly and didn't have any other symptoms except for a sore throat and hoarse voice, he allowed it.

After Marcus had given his statement to the police, the two of them started for home. Ricki held Lupo tightly in her arms. Marcus couldn't leave the little tomcat to an uncertain future and decided to take him home with them. He knew Brigitte wouldn't mind.

Ricki insisted that they stop at the paddock to say goodbye to Diablo first. He neighed happily and ran immediately to the fence when the girl called to him softly.

Officer Lester, who had stayed with the horses and was planning to spend the night with them, was relieved when Ricki confirmed that all the horses were accounted for. Now that the mystery of the saddled Diablo had been explained to him, he was glad that he had confiscated the saddle. He would see to it that the saddle was dusted for fingerprints in the morning.

"Diablo, you are an angel," whispered a worn-out Ricki, and she kissed her horse on the nose. "If it hadn't been for you, all of the horses would have burned to death, and Jake too. I hope he's beginning to feel better. Dad, can we stop by the hospital on the way home?"

Marcus shook his head firmly. "No, sweetheart. It's 3 a.m. Your mother has no idea what has happened and will be very worried—and anyway, you should be in bed. You're almost dead on your feet!"

Ricki nodded obediently, and let her father support her. She was truly at the end of her rope and just wanted to sleep. In the car she closed her eyes. Tears of exhaustion and fear rolled down her cheeks. Her skin looked as though it had been sunburned, and the doctor's salve did little to alleviate the discomfort it caused her. Her last wakeful thoughts were of Jake.

All the horses had escaped the fiery inferno, even Bronco and old Sugar had made it out safely, thanks to the intervention of the firemen. Now they stood with their fellow horses, somewhat confused but mostly unharmed.

No one—human or animal—had been seriously injured as a result of the fire, but it wasn't certain if Jake would survive this night.

As Marcus drove home in the darkness, an enormous sea of flames lit up the horizon. In spite of the heroic efforts of the firemen, by morning the former riding academy was reduced to debris and ashes.

*

Marcus carried Ricki into the house and explained briefly to the shocked Brigitte what had happened. Ricki's mother, full of gratitude that her loved ones had not been injured in the fire, sat down on the bed of her grimy, smoky daughter, who, with Lupo curled up in her arms, was sound asleep.

Ricki's father, however, went back to his car and drove to the hospital. He knew he wouldn't be able to rest until he found out how his friend Jake was doing.

In the Emergency Room, Marcus explained to the nurse that Jake didn't have any living relatives, but that he was an honorable member of the Sulai family. After some discussion, he found out that the old man was in the intensive care unit under constant observation.

Dr. Evans, the hospital's emergency room chief doctor, confirmed Dr. Kennedy's diagnosis. Jake had suffered a serious heart attack and, while he lay unconscious, smoke entered his lungs, making his condition worse. That he had even been able to speak was almost a miracle.

"I can't give you much hope," Dr. Evans said to Marcus outside the ICU. "But I'd say he has a 50-50 chance of survival if he makes it through the next 48 hours. At the moment, you can't do anything for him. I suggest you go home and get some rest. After everything that has happened, you could do with a little sleep. Perhaps I'll know more tomorrow."

Marcus nodded and firmly shook the doctor's hand before he dragged himself away, exhausted. At the exit door to the hospital, he leaned against the cool wall, stared at the sky, and took a few deep breaths.

He began to blame himself for not insisting that Jake see a doctor long ago, when he had first felt sick.

And he was also upset with himself that he hadn't taken Ricki's suspicions about the mysterious rider seriously. A boiling rage bubbled up inside him—both at himself and at the two arsonists whose deeds had endangered so many people and animals.

Furious, Marcus pounded his fist on the railing, but the pain that went through his hand didn't alleviate the pain in his heart.

*

"Ricki, you have company! Lillian Bates and Kevin are here!" Brigitte Sulai called softly through the door of her daughter's room. Ricki opened her eyes sleepily.

I overslept! was her first thought, but she saw by her alarm clock that it was 2:27 in the afternoon. Then she remembered her mother sent her back to bed this morning, after she had appeared in the kitchen about 9 a.m. and drank an enormous glass of orange juice. Despite a cold shower, she was still tired. Her throat still burned a little, and she felt more like a dried-out cactus than a human being.

Ricki looked toward the door, and the first thing she saw was a huge bouquet of flowers that was held out to her. Behind it, a pale Lillian beamed, followed by a limping Kevin, who was wearing a new walking cast.

Lillian embraced Ricki. "Thank you, thank you, thank you!" she blurted. "I am so grateful that Holli is still alive! And all the others, as well, of course. But Holli—well, you know! This morning the police telephoned all the members of the riding club, particularly the horse owners. It was Officer Fox who told us about what happened last night. My God, I'd just like to know what kind of a person could start that fire! How's Jake?"

Ricki shrugged. "I have no idea. He was still unconscious last night. Dad's going to drive to the hospital to see him again today."

Kevin nudged Lillian aside. "Make room for a poor invalid. Hello—how are you? I'm so relieved that nothing happened to you," he said, taking Ricki in his arms awkwardly, and giving her a hug. Since Mrs. Sulai and Lillian were in the room, he felt shy about giving Ricki a kiss. But his eyes spoke volumes.

"It's great to see you," she said warmly. "Wait, I'll get up and get dressed. We could go to see the horses—"

"Stop, young lady. Maybe it would be better if you—"

"But, Mom, after all the smoke I inhaled last night, I really need some fresh air, and I have to take care of Diablo. I hate to think of him standing outside with the others. If I only knew where I could put him for a while. I think the stable is completely destroyed."

"If my father weren't so stubborn, we could put him in

137

our stable," said Kevin, but he saw by the look on Ricki's face that that was the last place she would want to put her horse.

Lillian winked at her. "No problem," she said. "You know my parents have a farm, and after the events of last evening they decided to offer our barn as a temporary stable for all the homeless animals. It's only a provisional shelter, until they all find a place to go, but it's better than nothing, isn't it?"

"That's super! Tell them thanks a lot. When can we move in?"

Lillian grinned. "Should I reserve a little corner for you?"

"Why not? It'd be great to spend the night with 20 horses."

"You can still think about it. If you want, we could bring Holli and Diablo right over to my parents' place."

"Good, then just let me get dressed." She carefully pushed the blanket aside, awakening Lupo, who stretched and yawned a greeting to the guests.

"Does he belong to you now?" Lillian laughed.

"I think so. Common disasters form a bond!"

Kevin, looking a little forlorn, sat down on the edge of the bed and scratched the tomcat mindlessly. He would have loved to go with the two girls, but the cast on his leg prevented him from undertaking such a long trek.

"Well, then I guess I'll just limp back home," he said sadly. He had been so happy to see Ricki and had hoped they could spend the whole afternoon together. But he understood that first she had to take care of her horse and find a place for him to stay.

"How did you get here?" Mrs. Sulai pointed at his leg cast.

"Mom drove me. She said she'd pick me up after shopping, but if Ricki is leaving now, then—"

"Then you can either wait here, or I could drive you home, if you'd like."

"Mom, could you drive us and Kevin to the stable, or rather, what's left of it? We would ride the horses to Lillian's farm, and you could pick me up there." Then, turning to her friend, Ricki asked, "Lily, how long do you think it would take us?"

Lillian considered the question carefully. "Hmm … Holli can only walk slowly. So I think we should plan on 45 minutes."

Ricki's mother thought about it for a moment and then agreed.

"Okay, then that's what we'll do. I want to change my clothes, and Kevin, you can decide if you want to go with us, or if you want me to drive you home. Ricki, see if your brother would like to come with us."

Now Kevin's eyes were shining again. "No question, Mrs. Sulai. Of course, I'd like to go with them. I could call my mother on her cell phone."

"Okay, then do that now."

Brigitte and Kevin left the room while Ricki pulled on her riding jeans behind the screen.

"Ugh, you'd think I'd gained 20 pounds since yesterday," she groaned. "I can't believe it. I'll never be able to get in the saddle. Oh, the saddle," she suddenly remembered. "It's at the police station; I think the police want to check it for fingerprints."

Lillian made a face. "Be glad. Our saddles are all burnt up. So, are you ready?"

The two girls left Ricki's room and headed for the car. Brigitte was already behind the wheel, with the engine running.

On the way to the stable, Lillian asked Mrs. Sulai to stop

at the riding shop. She wanted to buy a replacement bit. Since she'd be getting her saddle and bit back in a few days, Ricki decided—just this once—to ride Diablo with a rope instead.

*

Brigitte, Harry, and Kevin turned pale when they saw what was left of the riding stable.

"Terrible," whispered Ricki's mother. She could hardly imagine what had happened the night before.

Ricki and Lillian were already on the way to their horses.

Ray Lester was still there and was very glad to see Ricki back to her old self.

"Hi, how are you?" he wanted to know. Ricki waved to him happily. "Good, thanks—and you?"

The policeman winked at her and laughed. "A shower wouldn't be amiss," he said while opening the gate to the paddock.

Diablo and Holli had seen their owners approach and came running. After a lot of hugging and stroking, both girls climbed onto the backs of the unsaddled horses. Lillian took one more look around.

"Several horses have already been picked up," she noticed, and Officer Lester informed them that the rest would be transported to their new stalls in trailers. "We have an agreement with the owners that the horses have to be loaded by 4 p.m."

"Well," said Ricki, "then hopefully you can go home soon."

Ray nodded and let the riders out of the paddock. Ricki waved one last time before Diablo and Holli moved off slowly.

140

Marcus paced back and forth nervously in the waiting room of the intensive care unit. He hoped to see Dr. Evans and get the latest news on Jake's condition. A heavy weight seemed to fall from his shoulders when the doctor reported that his friend's condition had stabilized and that he would be allowed a brief visit.

As Marcus entered Jake's hospital room, he could see that Jake had his eyes closed and was connected to various monitors and to devices with tubes. He spoke to him quietly, so he wouldn't be startled, and then put his hand on the old man's hand.

"You really gave us a scare," he said and smiled as Jake weakly turned to face him—still too exhausted to answer.

"You don't have to speak. Take your time."

Jake's lips formed the question, *Diablo?* and Marcus nodded reassuringly to calm his fears.

"Diablo and all the other horses are okay. We took Lupo home with us. Now if you just get better, everything will be fine."

Jake waved his hand feebly and turned his head away. He sensed that nothing would be okay for him again. After the fire there was nothing—neither his job nor his apartment—and he was practically helpless.

Maybe it would have been better if the doctors hadn't gone to so much trouble to bring me back to life. What kind of life is waiting for me now? wondered Jake, full of worry.

Marcus interpreted Jake's turning away as a sign of fatigue, so after promising to visit him again tomorrow, he quietly left the room.

*

"Are we all here?" Officer Clint Fox asked the members of the riding club who had assembled in the Bates family's machine shed. He had asked them to come not only to fill them in on the details of the fire but also to ask some questions and to take fingerprints.

He made a brief speech in which he outlined the facts of the case and told them that a broken kerosene lamp had been found that had probably caused the fire. Fox also mentioned that the main entrance key had been taken into custody, as well as the saddle of the horse that had been saddled that night, as they might have fingerprints on them that would point to the perpetrator.

"Since I don't believe that anyone here wanted to burn down the club's stable, you won't have anything to fear. I would like you to regard the fingerprinting as a purely routine measure that needs to be done in order to clear up this case."

Officer Fox stared penetratingly at each of the club members present. Some of them looked shocked or upset and uncooperative, but that was nothing new to the policeman.

As he got the list of the club members out of his briefcase, he didn't miss the fact that two people were moving unobtrusively behind the rest toward the door. They left the room secretively.

Look at that, Fox thought. *It seems the boy was right in his suspicions.*

Kevin, who had also observed the two, poked Ricki, nodded to the policeman, and then he and Ricki left the shed as well.

They noticed that the two got on their bikes quickly in order to flee. But Kevin, acting on instinct, had let the air out of their tires earlier, and the "getaway vehicles" were of no use.

"Where are you two going?" he called to the escapees, limping slowly toward them.

"We're done and we want to go home, but some jerk flattened our tires," one replied.

"So, some other jerks almost flattened Jake, 20 horses, and a cat! That's much worse than what happened to your bikes, don't you think?"

"What are you saying? It wasn't us, anyway!"

"Are you sure, Lark?" Ricki stepped forward from behind the bushes, startling her former girlfriend, who gaped in surprise.

Ricki looked at Lark with fixed eyes. "I believe this belongs to you, or am I wrong?" Ricki took the red and white headband out of her pocket and held it out to Lark.

"Where did you—?" Lark immediately realized that she had made a mistake and fell silent.

"Why are you limping?" asked Kevin, moving closer to Lark and forcing her to bump into her friend. Cathy winced. "And why does Cathy have a Band-Aid on her head?"

"That's none of your business!" replied Lark avoiding Ricki's eyes.

"Have you any idea how worried I was about Diablo? Do you know how Lillian felt the whole time? Do you even care that Jake had a heart attack and is in the intensive care unit? He lost the little possessions he had due to your stupidity. What were you thinking? Why did you do it?" Ricki spewed out her fury.

Cathy turned pale and started to shake all over. "We didn't do it on purpose! The lamp—it fell and—" she whimpered.

"Shut up!" Lark snapped. Then she turned defiantly to Ricki and Kevin. "We didn't do anything!"

143

"Lark, there's no point in lying anymore," Cathy, in resignation, tearfully pleaded, and she looked at Ricki with hurt and remorse in her eyes.

But Ricki felt only contempt for them. She threw the headband at Lark's feet and turned away, disgusted. "How could I ever have been so wrong about you two!"

"Ricki, please...we're sorry," Cathy said, her eyes downcast.

"I'm not sorry," said Lark, full of hate. "You didn't care about our friendship at all. Ever since you've had Diablo, we didn't count anymore. Suddenly, we weren't good enough for Miss Horse Owner!"

"Why do you say things you don't mean, things you know aren't true?" Kevin shook his head in bewilderment. "You hurt Ricki and others with your hostile behavior, do you know that? You used Diablo as an excuse to pay Ricki back for things that were your own fault. You were the one who didn't want the friendship to continue after Diablo changed owners. I'm pretty sure that you are behind all those nasty little things at school and that you are the one who started the ugly rumors that hurt Ricki so much. Even stealing money wasn't too much for you—"

"No," said Lark with a triumphant mean smile. "That was Sean!"

Cathy looked at Lark with dismay. Overcome with a heavy sense of guilt and regret that she had been a part of these awful events, Cathy slowly felt her courage return and confronted her partner in crime.

"Yeah, but only because you told him to. I should have never listened to you! The nightly rides—that was your idea. I don't know why you involved me in it. Just because you had to ride Diablo and were afraid to go alone, I had to go with you on Holli. If I had said no, you would have made my life just as miserable as you made Ricki's! But that wouldn't have been nearly as bad as what has happened now! I was such a coward. I hate you, Lark! I'm ashamed that I was ever your friend." Cathy turned her back on Lark.

"Thanks, that's enough. I don't think we've ever solved a case this quickly!" Clint Fox had followed them and heard everything.

"Thanks for the clue, my boy," he said to Kevin with an appreciative nod. Then, turning to Lark and Cathy, "Okay, you two, come with us," and he motioned the two girls toward the police car. "We're going to visit your parents. I imagine they will be delighted to hear the news about their daughters. By the way, Ricki, you can pick up your saddle and bit at the police station. We don't need them now. Well, see you."

"See you," said Kevin, and Ricki added, "I hope not!"

Together they watched the trio walk away until they disappeared in the police car.

"What did he mean 'clue'?" asked Ricki. Kevin put his arm around her and they started to walk to Lillian's house.

"I just put two and two together. Our first suspicions were confirmed faster than we thought, but at that time no one would have believed anything we said. After the fire, Fox was glad to listen to our theories, and I told him about them this morning."

*

"Jake will be released in one week," Ricki explained after she had been to see him at the hospital. "I think he feels better now than he ever did before."

145

"Good," said Brigitte, and exchanged knowing looks with her husband.

"Why are you looking at each other like that?" Harry asked, frightened that maybe his "Grandpa Jake" was not really better.

"Just wait! You'll find out soon enough," laughed Marcus, playfully grabbing his son for a hug.

"Parents are weird," grumbled the little boy, squirming away. "They always have secrets from their children!"

"No, no. We don't have any secrets from you. We wanted to talk with you anyway."

"Oh man," Ricki groaned. "That sounds like a family meeting. Did we do something wrong?"

"For once, no," answered Brigitte. "But we've been thinking about the addition to our family."

Both children's mouths dropped open with amazement.

"Brother or sister?" asked Ricki, regaining her composure.

"Neither," Brigitte laughed. "But if you are in agreement, and if one of you is willing to clear out his or her room temporarily and sleep on the couch, I could offer you a granddad. More precisely, we want to have Jake live with us, because he—"

Ricki and Harry were completely wild.

"Yeah! Cool! I can listen to his ghost stories every day, and he can tell me about Diablo, and he knows how to—"

"Slow down, Harry," Brigitte urged. "You know that he has been very sick and has to rest. That means we all have to be very considerate of him so that he can recuperate. When Jake moves in, that will be a big change for him and for all of us. After all, he has lived alone almost all his life, and we will have some adjustments as well."

Ricki and Harry looked at each other for a long time before Ricki said, "I'll sleep on the couch or in Harry's room in my sleeping bag. The main thing is that Jake will have a home again."

"Exactly!" Harry nodded in agreement.

Brigitte and Marcus were proud that their children immediately understood what the issue was really about. After the two had left to talk about it further, Marcus turned to his wife.

"So, that's cleared up! Now all we have to do is convince Jake. After all, we can't decide this without him."

Brigitte looked out of the living room window absently.

"I think he'll want to. Where else could he go?"

"Let's wait and see. It is and remains his own decision absolutely."

"Sometimes you have to force people to accept what's good for them," Ricki's mother said.

"Not Jake! His pride wouldn't allow it. But I think I know someone who could convince him."

*

During the next week, Ricki transferred most of her things into Harry's room, where he had willingly given her half of his shelves. After all, his sister had many cool things that he had wanted to have in his room for a long time.

Ricki took all the posters in her room off the wall except for the picture of a horse. She'd had a photo of Diablo enlarged and hung beside the dresser in a beautiful wooden frame. A bouquet of flowers decorated the small table that Brigitte had put in a corner of the room, along with two comfortable old armchairs. Several back issues of Ricki's *Horse and Rider* magazines were stacked neatly on the table's lower shelf.

147

Ricki's desk was now in Harry's room too, which was getting a little crowded. But the children didn't complain. They were excited that Jake would soon be moving in.

*

Several days later, in the afternoon, the doorbell rang at the Sulai home. Ricki, who opened the door, turned pale. There stood the two men whom she had unwittingly over-heard talking at the stable ages ago. The men who drove off in the big black limousine. They looked at the startled girl pleasantly.

"Are you Ricki?" asked one.

She could only nod.

"The Ricki who attempted to stop an animal abuser who had mistreated a horse and had to be admitted to the hospital afterward?" asked the second.

"Yeah, but—"

"Good, then we found the right place. My name is Tom Harvey," said the first man, "and this is Ed Turner." He pointed to the man who accompanied him.

"We are reporters for the animal-protection magazine *Animals Are Better Than People*, and we want to write an article about you. Is it true that the horse now belongs to you?"

Ricki took a deep breath. "I—"

"And why did the stable burn down? Is your horse still alive?"

"Maybe if you'd let my daughter speak, you'd have a chance to get your questions answered!" Brigitte had joined her daughter and opened the door a little wider. "And wouldn't it be more pleasant to talk over a cup of coffee than standing here at the door? Won't you come in?"

"Thank you, gladly."

For the next two hours the two men sat with Ricki and let her tell them the whole story while they made a lot of notes and asked a lot of questions. At the end of the interview, they were in agreement that Ricki and her horse were connected in a special way. They said she would be declared Animal Protector of the Year by their magazine, and her horse would be honored as a hero.

"Let us take a few photos of you and Diablo and then we'll leave you alone," laughed Tom Harvey. His colleague added, "You can read our article in a few weeks. We'll send you a copy of the magazine when the story comes out."

After saying their thank-yous and good-byes to Mrs. Sulai, they departed, leaving behind an excited—and very pleased—Ricki.

*

As promised, a copy of the magazine showed up in the mail several weeks later. Proudly Ricki showed the story about her and Diablo to her parents and Harry.

HERO ON FOUR HOOVES
The value of protecting animals, and how they thank you.
   Animal Protector of the Year, Ricki Sulai, tells the story of her horse, who once had been mistreated and now has saved lives.

Hopefully the whole envy thing won't start up all over again, thought Ricki while she imagined the reaction of the readers. But then she decided it was good that Diablo was being praised publicly. After all, it was he who had prevented anyone from getting hurt in the fire.

On the day of his release from the hospital, Jake sat on the edge of his bed, depressed. Beside him was a small travel bag filled with the few things Brigitte had brought him while he was in the hospital. All of his personal belongings had been destroyed in the fire. She had also brought him some clothes—all of them from her deceased father, who had been about the same size as Jake.

The old stable master glanced around the hospital room one last time. What would happen now? There was no place for him to go. Jake felt bitter and hopeless but as the door opened, and Harry rushed happily inside and hugged him, he forgot about his problems for the moment.

How often the little boy had listened so attentively when he told him ghost stories. Yes, the world had been a good place for him once. But now?

Jake didn't have any more time to think about it. Marcus came into the room behind his son and embraced his friend, who had risen stiffly. Taking Jake's bag, he led the old man to the door.

"Well, then, let's go! Be glad, that you're finally getting out of here! Brigitte baked a wonderful cake and the water for the coffee is already boiling—caffeine free, of course. We don't want you to have another attack!"

"And I painted a picture for you, but you'll get it afterward." Harry beamed at Jake, grabbed his hand, and pulled him outside.

All during the ride, Jake didn't say anything. Harry talked the whole time. Marcus knew he had made the right decision in taking his young son with him to pick up Jake from the hospital. As they were turning into the Sulai's street, Marcus let the car slowly roll to a stop.

Ricki and Brigitte were standing at the door, waving happily. And someone else was standing on the lawn, with a gleaming coat and arched neck. Diablo greeted his old friend with a loud whinny. The old man couldn't help but notice the large sign over the front door. He read it with tears in his eyes.

WELCOME HOME, GRANDPA JAKE

Harry couldn't wait to lead Jake into the house. "From now on you belong to us!" he declared, and Diablo reared up on his hind legs in agreement.